By

Tempie

PublishAmerica
Baltimore

First printing

At the specific preference of the author, PublishAmerica allowed this work to remain exactly as the author intended, verbatim, without editorial input.

ISBN: 1-4241-0706-7
PUBLISHED BY PUBLISHAMERICA, LLLP
www.publishamerica.com
Baltimore

Printed in the United States of America

Dedication

I dedicate this Novel to the loving memories of my parents, and my brother. I know they are each looking down from heaven now, and smiling. Mom, Dad, & my brother (Man), I'm smiling back. I love you and I hold sweet memories that will forever be in my heart. You know I really wrote this ten years ago, and I thank God he has allowed my dream to stay alive in my heart with you.

A special note to say thanks to my sister Lavern and my two nephews Christopher and Christian who brought so much joy to mom and dad in their last days on earth. My sister Lavern is the real hero in so many ways. It took a lot of love and sacrifice to take my mom and push her wheelchair and be her eyes so she could see and enjoy herself at Disney World. I still joke with her now in disbelief of her doing that but I'm so glad she did. I can just hear mom fussing and her pushing now…smile. I also am glad she kept cooking and barbecuing dad's favorite dishes so he ate them. No matter how mad he made her, she never stopped. Lastly, a special note of appreciation to my sister Lavern who does so much behind the scene and doesn't talk about it like me…smile.

Without her love, encouragement and taking care of me these past couple of years, and insisting I follow my dreams I could never have finished writing this Novel. You have been my big sister! I love You and I Thank You! Mom and Dad are proud of you also!

A note to the memories of all who loss their lives from the hurricane Katrina and may a beacon of light and a ray of hope always shine in the hearts of those left behind.

Acknowledgments

First giving all honor to God!!!

Philippians 4:13—I can do all things through Christ which strengtheneth me.

I thank God for his favor and blessings in allowing all of the love, support, encouragement and prayers of so many people. There is no way I can list everyone by name but just know you are in my heart.

In naming a few, my sincere thanks to all of my family including Lavern, Christopher, Christian, Regina, Andre', Keith Andre', Samuel, Laverne, Martez, the newlyweds—Crystal & Curtis.

Also, Almeta & John Lee, Mae, Bro & Irene and a host of other relatives and friends.

Thanks to Pastor Randy & Sister Donna and all of my Church Road Baptist Church members.

Thanks to Rev. Hayes and all of Greater Lakeview Baptist Church members including the Deacon Board and Bro. Shorter. Thanks to all of the other churches my family and I have attended and belonged to through the years including Trinity Church and Moody Church in Chicago, IL.

Thanks to Kathy and all of my childhood friends and neighbors. Also, Doris & Sinclair, Juanita & Earl, Lucius & Mattie Mae, Alice & Brent, Wayne & Pat, Cheryl & Billy, James & Henrietta.

Thanks to Cathy and all of my college friends. Thanks to Willie Mae, Bryce, Charles.

Thanks to Mr. Tasic and all of my hospital, laboratory and nursing home friends. Also, Mary, Barb, Jane, Janice, Bridgette, Richard, Millie, Craig, Angie, Ozella, Verdie, Louise, and many others. Also thanks to my many friends on the various jobs I have worked. Thanks to Adrienne, Raven, Robert, Jean Marie, Mary, Ronald, Victor. Also thanks to Marilyn.

Thanks to Viola, Nancy, Dorothy, Jennie, Selena, Janice, Terry, Jeff, Paula, Bobby, Jon, Jamie, Ryan, Bob, Mike, Sally, Beverly, Kathie, Thuy, Angela, Shirley and all of my support groups and friends. Thanks to Ken & Susan.

Thanks to Alisha, Sherita, Shelia, Felecia, Dorothy, Donna, April, Deborah, Dot, Kendra, Tasha, Tanja,Camela, and Roufie. Thanks to Tee, LaShaunda, Sabra, Robin, Brenda, Cindy, Bonnie, Cydney, Barbara, Emanuel, DavidR, Gena, Teresa, Lucinda, DavidL, Saundra,Jean, Tim, Bob, Meg, Joy, MacKenzie, Dian, Ethylene, Mark and all of my other book club and blogging friends and authors.

Thanks to Publish America for believing in me and my work! You not only gave me a contract and agreed to publish my work; you help make a ten year dream come true for me and took a chance on an unknown author publishing my first of many Novels…

Chapter One

Excuse Me, Do I Know You? Memphis, Tennessee, 1977

One pair of medium brown eyes opened wide and ready to see the world; and one pair of dark brown eyes faintly teary and struggling to stay open. Noise was all around but neither could hear anything. Both seemed to have been frozen in the moment. One knowing something had to be done soon and one knowing each second that passed would never return.

As moments went by...

"Hang in there! My unknown friend, the doctor will be in here shortly," Manerva seemed to say with sharpness in her eyes as she looked up to see that the time was 5:15pm on the large white clock hanging on the wall above her bed. Walking over closer, she noticed this person lying almost lifeless on her back. Her arms were just hanging on both sides of the bed. Her head was slightly tilted back with no movement.

Yet with her eyes, she seemed to be reaching out to Manerva, with every bit of desire to live.

"Will you please help me, please? I need you!" her silent tears seem to say as they fell slowly from her big dark brown eyes. Her skin and hair was a shade even darker. This was a noticeable contrast from

Manerva's medium light brown skin tone. Eyes that didn't seem to blink but somehow moved with Manerva's movement.

"Do I know you? Do you know me? Where is the Doctor? Where is someone to help you?" Manerva thought these questions out loud.

As Manerva moved those dark brown eyes moved with her every step...

Even though Manerva kept waiting and looking around the dimly lit room; she could still feel the gentle warmth from within the darkness. *Warmth from her moving eyes. Warmth from her desire to live.* Not understanding why but gently and softly taking a kleenex and wiping each tear as quietly as they fell.

Here both women were, this steaming hot summer evening in room number one at First General Hospital's Emergency Room, chanced by a situation that could bring them back together many years later.

Knock! Knock! Then suddenly...

The door was pushed opened by a tall young man, with a neatly cut afro, wearing eyeglasses, a white medium length lab coat over a pair of blue hospital scrubs rushed past Manerva. He placed his red lab tray with different colored test tubes and needles on the corner of the cabinet top next to the glass jars that was filled with cotton balls and Q-tip swabs. On the shelves beneath were hospital gowns, bed pads, towels, linens, and everything else that was needed in an emergency room.

"I'm from the laboratory, my name is Bates and I'm here to draw blood from you," He quickly announced.

Manerva watched both the lab technician and the patient's responses very closely. She noticed it became obvious to him immediately, that the patient was in pain and had difficulty moving her body. She gave a quick glance at the same white clock hanging over her bed and noticed ten more minutes had passed. It was becoming harder and harder by the moment to just wait and watch her suffer so.

"Follow your instructions, just wait, he may have ordered the lab tech to come in first, just wait Manerva," this voice inside of her kept saying.

Bates reached into his red lab tray and removed a pair of gloves and a tourniquet. Skillfully, placing the tourniquet across his right shoulder while bending down, he checked the patient's armband to see what her name was. Afterwards, he grabbed his red lab tray, walked on the other side of her bed and slowly stretched out her left arm.

"Roberta, I'm going to tie this tourniquet just above your left elbow, can you make a fist for me with your left hand?"

Manerva saw she was trying and struggling very hard just to close her hand. As she walked over to the left side of Roberta to help, Bates had gently helped close her fist while smiling as he gave a couple of thumps on her skin.

"It's going to be a little stick. You've got a good vein here; try not to move this arm. I'm going to use what we call a butterfly needle, you will feel a small pinch and it will all be over," he said, getting the four test tubes, an alcohol packet, a cotton ball and a band aid and placing them in his pocket from his red lab tray.

Manerva didn't move or seem to blink an eye as she watched. She made sure she was out of his way and politely watched.

"He's got to be wondering who am I and why am I not helping this patient more."

Bates then inserted the different test tubes into the barrier of the butterfly, one by one, first the large clear red tube, then the short lavender tube, then the red tube with the gel at the bottom, and lastly the short blue tube. Between inserting each tube he quickly glanced over to see Manerva carefully watching him and Roberta while looking around the room.

She looked at everything; from the green and silver oxygen tank sitting on the left of the bed to the red crash cart sitting to the right. She had already washed her hands and had her gloves on before he had entered the room.

He knew she had been startled and disappointed in disbelief when the door opened and it was him and not the intern she had been waiting for. He sensed she felt he was doing a good job with the patient but could hardly just keep waiting and watching knowing Roberta was in so much agony and pain. Bates was touched because of the compassion this young medical student had. He knew she was totally unaware of what was happening. For a brief moment he thought maybe they know one another.

"Excuse me but would you mind passing me another one of those large clear red tubes from my tray, please?" he asked noticing Manerva had moved over to the side close to his lab tray never taking her eyes off of the Roberta.

"Sure."

"Here it is. I'm sorry, my name is Manerva," she said as she handed him the tube.

"Don't worry about it; I saw it on your ID badge."

"Is that all you need from your tray?" she asked.

"I hope so," Bates said as he too had noticed Roberta's struggling was becoming less and less apparent.

Quickly analyzing the situation without breaking his routine he looked over to Manerva.

"After doing this for almost twenty years, some things you just know and especially in room number one of this emergency department.

"It is to always get enough blood, because sure enough, time you get back to the lab, they will page you right back. And I don't like sticking people more than once, if I can help it."

"I always treat people like I want to be treated."

"Plus if someone sticks me with a needle, I sure hope they got all they need the first time!"

"Also, as I passed the nurses station I overheard them talking about a hit and run victim being treated," Bates said while finishing up and labeling all of the tubes.

Bates carefully discarded his needle in the biohazard container mounted on the wall and placed all of his waste paper items and gloves in the trash can underneath. Manerva saw the pride he took in his work, even in how he washed his hands.

"Thanks for doing such a professional job," Manerva said.

"Oh, this is nothing," he repeated.

"I can do this with my eyes closed."

"Which Intern are you observing?" he asked Manerva, as he picked up his red lab tray preparing to leave the room.

"How did you know, I'm a medical student?" she asked.

"Like I said, I've been doing this almost twenty years, you just learn."

"And besides, I saw Dr. Grant sitting with his feet propped up bragging as usual when I passed the nurses station coming into this room."

"I noticed you've been in here alone just waiting, I just put two and two together."

"Everybody know that's his style."

"He just leaves the medical student in the room and let them wait."

"It's all a game to him."

"He calls it your initiation period."

"Happens over and over, but nobody does anything about it," he seem to chuckle as he was leaving.

"You just have to do your job, if you want to survive around here and hope you don't run into Dr. Grant."

"Just remember he could care less about anyone, other than himself," he stated just as the door closed behind him.

You see, Manerva was a beginning third year medical student. Even though she had always been one of the tops in her class, she couldn't deny the uneasiness she was feeling now. This was her first emergency room rotation, and she had been assigned to observe and rotate with the in-house intern. She just had no idea the in-house intern would be Dr. Grant. Rubbing her sweaty palms together and walking across the room turning toward the door, wondering while inwardly gritting her teeth.

"How long can this patient hold on?"

"I should just go to the nurse's station and get him myself."

She knew that was too easy and that this was just a test for her. Bates was absolutely correct.

He's just waiting to see my reaction. My instructions were to be inside room one at 5:00pm and wait; the intern would already be inside with the patient.

Just then she heard another male voice speaking as he entered the room...

"I need an EKG, blood gases and blood cultures times 30 minutes apart."

"The routine blood work has already been drawn by lab."

"X-Rays have already been done also," he said while giving Manerva a repulsive stare.

"Yes doctor," the nurse quickly said, who had walked into the room with him, as he handed her the patient's chart.

"Nurse, also page the admitting staff surgeon and have him come examine and confirm my diagnosis immediately."

"Have blood bank on stand by in case we need a type and cross match, for a transfusion."

"This patient may have some internal bleeding," he said as he continued checking her vitals.

"Yes, Dr. Grant," the nurse said, after glancing up and checking his name on his badge.

Manerva, walked out of the room with the intern, never taking her eyes off of the patient, still lying on the hospital bed, *only now her big dark brown eyes were closed.*

A brief second went by then out of no where came

"You were late!" Dr. Grant stated.

Then almost immediately following with the same tone of harshness came...

"Is this your first observation," he asked in the same harsh tone as if to get Manerva's attention. He then just stood in the hallway outside of room number one, with tall broad shoulders standing at attention waiting for Manerva's response.

Without holding back came...

"Late!" Manerva said as if invisible venom of rage squirted from her nostrils.

She quickly composed herself and spoke while noticing his name as the nurse had earlier on his badge. He had never introduced herself and at this point it didn't matter. Calmly and collectively Manerva looked him straight into his eyes.

"Dr. Grant my instructions from the Dean of Students were to go into room number one of this emergency department at 5:00pm and the in-house intern I had been chosen to observe would already be there!"

"I was also told to just wait inside the room and observe everything."

"I have been waiting inside room number one since 5:00pm!"

Not allowing Manerva to say another word...

Dr Grant immediately interrupted and with a pronounced rudeness almost at a shout.

"Lesson number one, if you are to observe and rotate with me young lady is too always be on time."

"And on time in my book, is always thirty minutes earlier than told!"

"This is something you should already know!"

"I performed my differential diagnosis on the patient in room number one and had been waiting on you since before 4:30pm."

"Now, that we have an understanding about that young lady, answer my next question."

"Is this your first emergency room rotation and observation?"

Manerva was simply in disbelief of this entire conversation, but managed to keep her self-control and answered back.

"Dr. Grant, I've observed rotations in ICU, CCU, and Pediatrics and have had a lot of emergency training in taking care of all different kind of trauma patients. She said that with increased rage inside as she walked vigorously down the hallway trying to keep up with him as he had turned and walked away.

Suddenly he stopped dead in his tracks, and turned around, saying to her face

"So the correct answer to my question should be.

"Yes, Dr. Grant, this is my first emergency room rotation."

Face to face, looking her straight in the eye, while shaking his shoulder length blonde hair and flopping it all around as if to purposely have it fall near her face spoke as unsympathetically as possible.

"During my observation, if you really want to learn, I suggest you first of all be on time, take mental notes of everything I do, don't question my actions, and stay out of my way."

"I've been doing this longer than you, and will probably be here well after you are gone."

"I was the best intern and resident in my class and I specialized in emergency medicine, that's why I'm the emergency room in-house physician tonight. Simply put.

"I'm the best here."

"Do I make myself clear!" he asked insensitively.

Manerva was almost shaking to keep her composure trying to avoid reaching her boiling point while biting her top lip to keep from slapping him at that very moment. Managing to just say with sureness in her voice.

"Yes, Dr. Grant, I understand completely."

"Good, then we should have a smooth rotation."

It became very apparent, very quickly that the most important thing to Dr. Grant was his establishment of:

"I am the boss!"

"I am in total control!"

"My way or No way!"

Manerva was appalled to say the least! Not that Dr. Grant was a pompous and arrogate bully trying to play mind games but that he had no concern of the patient still lying in room number room *now with her eyes closed.* That didn't even bother her as much as trying to imagine the level of care or bedside manner Dr. Grant had given the patient with the dark brown eyes.

"He had set the whole thing up."

"He had purposely been in Roberta's room, before she had arrived at 5:00pm."

"Performed a quick diagnosis, and really that was it!"

"He didn't treat her trauma any more serious than he would have had he passed a dog lying in the street after being hit by a car."

In fact, according to all the rumors she had heard, *the dog would probably have gotten better treatment as long as it wasn't black or a female.*

"That's why Roberta was pleading with me with her eyes!"

"She knew!"

"She was begging for help!"

"What should I have done?"

All of these thoughts went racing in Manerva's mind. She had to get a grip of herself and quick. She had to do her job. She had to do what was best.

Manerva remembered the lab technician and all of what he had said...

She wasn't sure but she figured Dr. Grant had to be no more than thirty years old, but the rumors she had heard about him as well as the behavior she had witnessed of him and his bedside manner with patients and staff as well as with herself, mimicked some old southern plantation owner you read about or have heard your grandparents talk about. Manerva had been born and raised in Memphis, TN. She was very proud of her southern upbringing. Both her parents were born and raised in the south. In her lifetime, she had witnessed some of history's most memorable events involving the Civil Rights Movement especially when Dr. Martin Luther King visited Memphis; but in all her days, she had not experienced how Dr. Grant tried to make her feel at that very moment. She summed him up.

"A total jerk!" she thought.

Anger still was building inside of her with how indifferent he was with her and how hardhearted he had been with his patients.

"Who does he think he is?"

"How can he be so heartless?"

"If only you could read my mind and know what I really want to tell you!"

Manerva was thinking in her mind. She knew his report would weigh heavily toward her final grade. She already knew whatever report he would turn in on her would not be good.

"Bates had already warned me."

"Sadly, all of my hard work really won't matter."

Frequent thoughts went running through her mind a mile a minute, as she kept herself composed, while still looking into Dr. Grants piercing eyes. She was determined to brush away any emotion that showed in her eyes toward him. She had worked too hard to get where she was; and the most important matter at hand was hoping all was well with his patients. She had heard many rumors about him and had hoped she would observe another intern. But that didn't happen; she was stuck with Dr. Grant.

"He was nothing but an arrogant, pompous, male chauvinist pig and a racially prejudiced womanizer in her opinion."

She had often heard other medical students say similar things. Her roommate had even mentioned over lunch one day what she had heard.

"He hated blacks and felt medical school was no place for women especially no black woman."

The fact was now she knew all the rumors she had heard about him were true without any doubt. Additionally, it had been said all over the hospital.

"He got away with everything because he was the son of one of the wealthiest Board of Trustee Members at First General Hospital."

She noticed how busy the emergency room was and even though

she continued with Dr. Grant and observed many different trauma patients, she couldn't stop thinking about the patient with the dark brown closed eyes.

Over an hour had passed...

As Dr. Grant sat at the nurses' station looking through the charts, he asked the nurse sitting next to him.

"Where are the lab results and the admitting staff doctor's diagnosis for the patient in room number one?"

The nurse looked twice in the chart; looked up and responded back.

"All of the lab results are not in the charts and there is no diagnosis written by the admitting staff doctor either?"

"I know that, where are they he shouted!"

Manerva quickly stepped out of the way...

"Charge Nurse, please come to the nurses station!" was immediately heard overhead.

"What!" Dr. Grant shouted.

"Forget charge nurse, page the admitting staff doctor STAT!"

"Get blood bank here STAT!"

"Let's get this patient prepped for surgery, STAT!"

Manerva sensed the sudden urgency of all...

She saw people rushing in and out of room number one. Within minutes later, the admitting staff doctor came running. He grabbed the chart and looked at it. He quickly saw the differential diagnosis Dr. Grant had written awaiting his supervision and most likely diagnosis. He then slammed the chart down, and rushed into room number one.

"I'm Dr. Mahoney, step aside."

He examined the patient immediately noticing severe symptoms of pain and discomfort. Within minutes he shouted.

"Let's get this patient to surgery STAT!"

"Give her four units of blood STAT!"

"Where are all the lab results?"

"Who is this patient's nurse?"

"Where it she?" he asked.

Manerva again felt so helpless, *there was no longer warmth in this room, now only fear.* She realized she should be observing Dr. Grant but at that moment she didn't care, she had looked over and noticed those big dark eyes that were once faintly opened *now remained close.*

She walked over closer to the bed as they were about to wheel her out to surgery and with her eyes teary, she whispered again in silence.

"Hang on my unknown friend; please open your eyes again!"

Manerva whispered this but deep in her heart she *knew they would never open again*; she knew it was *too late.*

In all the commotion, Manerva walked over while Dr. Grant, Dr. Mahoney and the nursing staff were all talking at the nurse's station and no one was looking *She glanced at her chart.*

"So Roberta, you are twenty one"

"Five feet three inches tall"

"Weigh one hundred thirty pounds"

"Single"

"No children"

"And a nursing student"

As Manerva stood there glancing at her chart, those were the only statistics that mattered to her.

Pondering over and over in her mind...

"Why do I feel as though I know you?"

"I know we have never met."

"Yet when I first looked into your eyes."

"It took me back feeling as though we had met?"

"Feeling that it was not by chance that we were alone in that room."

"Feeling you wanted me to know something."

"I only wish I knew what?"

"I only know we are about the same age and even though I never have had a desire to go to nursing school my parents; especially my father's biggest dream for me is to become a doctor."

"And so I am."

"I wonder do you have parents like that?"

"Roberta, are your parents here?"

"I haven't seen anyone come in this room or ask about you at the nurses' station. If so, and they are here; where are they now?

"According to your chart and the rumors, it was hit and run."

"How could someone just hit you and leave you like this?"

"Why am I thinking about all this at a time like this?"

"I just hope when you return from surgery your eyes are open and you are better."

A loud voice shouted out...

"Young Lady!"

"Where were you just now?

Recognizing immediately that it was Dr. Grant's voice, I said...

"Manerva, my name is Manerva R. Jones, Dr. Grant and I'm fine."

"Do you know how the patient from room number one is doing in surgery?"

"Well now, Ms. Jones, the answer is No!"

"I know nothing further about how the patient is doing in surgery."

"It's going to be awhile because she had to be given four units of blood."

"And afterwards if all goes well, she will go to recovery."

"Anyway, she is Dr. Mahoney's patient now. If there are any complications, I'll be the first to hear about it," he answered all with an uncaring tone.

"A gunshot victim was just taken to room number one, we need to go!" he said very adamantly.

"Dr. Grant, its 10:30pm, I've been in classes since 6:00 this morning, you may not care but I need to stop and eat something. I have been with you all evening for five and a half hours without a five minute break!" Manerva said at this point not caring how he responded.

"Well, young lady, I will go see about the gunshot victim now in room number one, I'll see you at 6:00am tomorrow morning in room number one, and make sure you eat something first!" he said as he turned and walked away.

Manerva was hungry but sighed a moment of relief...

"This night is not over. I'm going to eat something and then find out how Roberta is doing? I'm not leaving here until I do!" she thought out loud.

With all of the trauma patients she had observed and witnessed, she wanted to think this night was almost over. But she knew it was just the beginning. She just didn't know of what. She watched and took mental notes all evening of Dr. Grant. His actions were completely different with certain patients. A few he was even cordial with. He had conversation with some of the patient's family member's and acted as if he cared.

"But with Roberta, there was nothing! He just seems to act as if she still doesn't exist. I just wish I had seen him in the room with her when he examined her. I know she was trying to tell me something. If I had only found out what it was," Manerva just couldn't stop thinking about everything.

She was beginning to blame herself again for not doing more. Feeling helpless and powerless was all in her eyes. Could she have rushed Dr. Grant? With all the time that had passed, could she have reminded Dr. Grant to make sure the admitting staff doctor had diagnosed Roberta? Or should she have taken it upon herself to go through Roberta's chart and make sure all her lab results were there? Questions, questions, questions and what were the answers.

Realizing she had somehow wondered into the hospital cafeteria, maybe because after leaving Dr. Grant and getting off the elevator on

the second floor, she could smell the aroma o'
For just a brief moment Manerva stood ther
savor all of what she was smelling.

She smiled...

This was the first time she could remember feeling a se... anything good since she had been on rotation with Dr. Grant. She looked over and saw there was not a long line at the food counter either.

"This is exactly what I need, some good home cooked food."

"No more vending machine snacks."

"At least not now," sighing in relief while looking up at the hospital cafeteria menu.

"I'd like some macaroni and cheese, a BLT on wheat bread with mayonnaise and what kind of soup is that?" she looked up and asked the older lady that was serving food behind the counter.

"Oh, that's fresh vegetable soup; it was just made about fifteen minutes ago when the shift changed. And it's good, I just had some, let me fix you a bowl, you look like you could use it," the older lady with the friendly smile and a consoling tone said to Manerva.

"Yes ma'am I can, thanks!" Manerva answered back smiling.

As she showed her ID badge to the cashier to pay for her food and receive her student discount, she asked him,

"Will I be able to hear all of the hospital pages if I sit in that room over to the left?"

"No, there is just a house phone for calling out on the wall in that room, but if you go to the conference room straight back you can," the cashier said.

While walking toward the back she passed a couple of tables and she saw a couple of her classmates that occasionally she would stop and talk to; but not now, she needed to be alone. She just wanted to enjoy her food and try to figure out what to do next. She had to reflect and stay focused.

This cafeteria was a community in itself. It had just been

eled two weeks prior. First General Hospital was located in the dical Center Loop Area. There were five other hospitals and six ge professional office buildings within this two mile area. This area was located three miles from the downtown Memphis and Mississippi River Front. People came here from all around. Everybody had been talking about how three of the five hospitals and three of the large professional office buildings had just been bought out by Resurrection Charities. This was a very powerful network of businessmen who had come to Memphis a year prior for the sole purpose of Business Developments.

Manerva couldn't wait to sit down and force herself to eat. *She smiled again.* The aroma inside the entire cafeteria smelled so good! It reminded her of a lot of days she had to study for a test or just wanted to think straight. Or when she ate some of her mother's good old fashioned country cooking and felt so on top of things. Now, this was one of those times.

Only this time it was for someone other than herself. *She needed strength and solace for her unknown friend with the dark brown eyes.*

"She had to eat enough for her!"

"She had to do it now!"

"Her strength would be Roberta's!"

"They would be one!"

"Manerva would be Roberta!"

Manerva found the perfect table...

Just across from the magazine and newspaper racks. She sat in the chair closest to the window. As she was walking to that table she could catch a quick glance at the view.

On the other side of the room were two older doctors talking. They appeared relaxed and enjoying whatever conversation they were engaged in. Both were smiling and laughing. Both of their plates were completely empty also. Manerva came to the conclusion that they had enjoyed whatever food they had.

The menu had a variety of foods but she had chosen to eat as light as possible and still eat enough because her night was not over. She had debated in her mind.

"Should I get the fried catfish and slaw."

"Or the roast beef and mashed potatoes and gravy."

"Or even the turkey and dressing."

She was satisfied at what she had decided to get with the help of the nice lady that served her the soup and BLT sandwich.

"It was exactly right!"

"This soup taste good, almost like my mama's!"

"It feels so good going down!"

Manerva thought while savoring her last spoonful as she looked out the window feeling the effect of a beautiful full moon glowing on a clear summer night. At that very moment as Manerva rubbed her forehead with her fingers relieving the tension and resting her elbows on the table looking up and out onto the newspaper stand to her left she saw something.

She had to open her eyes wider and blink a couple of times....

"Am I seeing straight?"

"It can't be!"

"It just can't be!" she said sadly to herself as she walked over to take a closer look.

But there it was, bold and bright, front page news! It even had a portrait of the entire family!

How could this be...

Hospital Board of Trustee...Memphis New Candidate for Mayor!!!

Dr. Henry T. Grant Sr.

(Grandson of the late Cotton Tycoon—Mitchell D. Grant)

Chapter Two

All That Matters!

"I feel more powerless than ever now and there is no way I want to take a chance of running into Dr. Grant anymore tonight. I will get enough of him again tomorrow morning. It's obvious that even if he did know anything about Roberta's condition he would never tell me. I could go up to surgery, but I don't know exactly how much power he has there either and especially after reading that his father is running for Mayor of the City, No, I've just got to find out what I need to know in my own way, just think Manerva think!" She thought out loud as she placed her empty dishes and tray on the conveyor belt, while walking toward the exit doors of the cafeteria.

A voice from behind...

"Hey student Doc, you sure put in long hours!"

Manerva quickly turned around to see it was the nice lab technician, Bates. He had just come into the cafeteria from an inside door which went straight up to the seventh floor of the hospital.

"You too!" she said.

"Yeah, but not for long, I'm working a double shift because we are short staffed, so I'm going to use one of the empty rooms on seven south to sleep a couple of hours, shower and change. I just came down to grab a bit to eat," Bates explained while looking down at Manerva's empty plate.

"I see your plate is clean. I can't wait to clean mine. I could smell the food coming down the back stairs. Since all the changes and remodeling has been going on, the food has been much better. The food doesn't taste like hospital food now and it's cooked fresh throughout the night now. My regular shift is eleven to seven in the morning; they had called me in to work three to eleven today and I need the money!" he said, as he picked up a copy of a newspaper lying on the table by the door.

"So it is true."

"Everybody is talking about it."

"So, his old man is running for Mayor."

"I guess that's good and bad for us!" Bates said while shaking his head.

"What do you mean by that," asked Manerva.

"Well, the good thing is that we will be getting the best of everything here as far as equipment and all, but the bad thing is that if you ain't part of the in crowd you better watch yo back, cause you won't be here long! I know I shouldn't say that, but I've been here too long. No one will ever say it but if you ain't in the right crowd you want have a chance. And you know from today who is not in the right crowd. The even sadder thing is we have a lot of good people here, staff and patients but it won't matter if people like Dr. Grant stay in power! I hear his father isn't so bad, it's just him. I know a lot of stories that should have made headline news in the paper just like this, but they never will." he said hurriedly.

"Got to go, Doc, will you be in the emergency room again tomorrow?" he asked as he walked toward the food counter and Manerva placed her dishes and tray on the conveyor belt.

"Sure thing, bright and early at 6:00am! Have you heard anything about that young lady patient that was in room number one when I met you earlier?" asked Manerva.

"Well, you didn't hear it from me, but I did over hear a couple of the med techs in the lab talking about the patient in room number one's urine test showed she was pregnant."

"Pregnant!" repeated Manerva.

"That was no where in her chart! Bates, do you know where she is? Is she still in surgery? Does she have family here?" Manerva asked.

"I don't know but why don't you go to the surgery waiting room and see for yourself? You will probably find out more there than you will from Dr. Grant, and if you mention to anyone you are observing him in rotation, everybody will be as quiet as a mouse, in fear of their job! Like I said, you didn't hear that from me! OK," said Bates with a look of anticipation in his eyes as he said it.

"OK, thanks and you didn't tell me anything," Manerva said back with a gleam of hope in her eyes.

As the elevator doors opened...

Manerva got off and walked pass the front desk with the hospital volunteer wearing a candy stripe red and white pinafore outfit over a white nurse's dress sitting at it. The volunteer seemed to be in her late sixties. She wore her hair neatly pinned up, and greeted Manerva with a warm smile.

"You student doctors sure work late and hard!" she said.

For a brief second Manerva seemed a bit startled until she quickly remembered she still had on her white lab coat and medical student ID badge and she had to think fast.

"Yes, I'm on my way back to the dorm and I wanted to check in the waiting room to see if my roommate was here. I think she was rotating through surgery and recovery."

"Do you know the intern's name she would be with? I can check the board or have them paged?" the volunteer asked?"

"No, don't bother, it's late, she may be gone, I'll just walk through and get a cup of that fresh coffee I smell brewing," said Manerva.

"I just put that pot of coffee on because there is a family in the waiting room that has been waiting all evening and still no word about their daughter that is in critical condition. They say she was involved in a hit and run accident just outside the hospital. Talk is she is a nursing student and was walking from the out patient building just across the walk way from the emergency room. They say she lost so much blood; her count was too low to do surgery. Her family is very upset with the doctors because they were not notified earlier and when they got to the hospital the patient was in a coma. I overheard some of the talk that the patient stayed in the emergency department way too long. Also, I don't know if you were out in that hot heat today, but it got up to 103 degrees outside about the same time they say some car hit her, and she fell and must have rolled on the side of a parked car by the sidewalk. Can you believe someone just left her there!" the volunteer said as she walked over to one of the pay telephones hanging on the wall to answer that had been ringing.

As Manerva walked through the waiting room, she looked to her right. There were about eight people all in the same section. Everybody was crying and hugging one another. An older woman was sitting next to the man sitting in the large reclining chair in a wheelchair. It appeared she was blind, because a young female teenager was feeding her what appeared to be soup from a bowl. There were two couples standing around the older women in the wheelchair. There was another male teenager sitting back and staring out the window that was facing the outside. There were no other people in the waiting room. All eyes quickly looked up at Manerva when she walked into the room. She realized they were each on pins waiting to hear from the doctors about Roberta's condition.

Manerva, at that moment, with all that she had in her managed to just walk through with a warm and sincere look on her face. As she reached the kitchen area all she could do was sit in the chair next to the counter and wait as the coffee slowly filled in the pot. She realized there was nothing she could say but she wanted to do or say something to connect to Roberta's family, to the family of her dark brown eyed friend. She slowly got up and went back through the door which went from the kitchen area.

Step by step...

She came closer to their section, and asked in a sincere whisper.

"Would anyone like me to fix them a hot fresh cup of coffee."

The man sitting in the recliner next to the older woman in the wheelchair politely answered.

"Yes, thank you, I'll take a cup, black please!"

"The older women in the wheelchair, looked up, to see, and asked in a soft voice.

"Are you a doctor honey?"

"How is my grandbaby?"

"How is Roberta?"

"Can you tell us anything? I can't see, but I can hear, so tell me please!" She kept repeating in as she began to cry with her last word.

"She'll be alright grandma!" said the teenager feeding her.

"Yeah, grandma, remember what you always tell us about, how God works in mysterious ways," said the male teenager as he walked over and put his arms around her neck.

"Doctor, can you tell us anything!" one of the women in the couple asked.

"I'm so sorry I can't tell you anything, I'm only a medical student, but I'm sure someone will tell you something as soon as they can. I know that is not what you need to hear, but try to stay encouraged," Manerva said as she turned back around toward the kitchen to get the cup of coffee.

As she walked into the kitchen...

She rested her hands on the counter and reached up to wipe the tears that were slowly trickling down her face listening to the soft spiritual music being played on the waiting room overhead intercom system. After a few moments she composed herself, and as she was about to step outside the kitchen area door back into the waiting room with the fresh brewed cup of coffee she had fixed before she heard loud talking and crying on the other side of the door.

She waited at the doorway inside because they had all moved just outside the kitchen door when two doctors wearing surgical outfits walked into the room from the kitchen area where Manerva was.

"I'm Dr. Mahoney and this is Dr. Campling. We've just finished surgery. Roberta is in recovery right now. We can't make any promises because we just don't know. This was a very complex surgery, because Roberta had lost so much blood. We gave her units of blood, but it appeared her body was not compatible. Her body reacted unfavorable so we had to stop the transfusions. All of her vital signs did not support the surgery she needed to have done. The only other alternative was to call in Dr. Campling, who is the best in his field to perform laser surgery. This we felt would off set some of the reactions that were being caused by the blood reactions. At this point we do not know the outcome. Only time will tell. Roberta is still not responding on her own. We have her on a respirator and are giving her several medications. I'm sorry, I wish we had more we could tell you," Dr. Mahoney said.

"We have done all we can do, she has suffered a lot of internal bleeding; now it's up to God. We are closely monitoring Roberta throughout the night, as soon as we know something, we will let you know," Dr. Campling said and then asked.

"Is there anything you all want to know that we may not have covered?"

Getting weak to her knees...

Manerva slowly set both the cups of coffee she held in both her shaking hands as she looked back and sat down in one of the chairs at a table by the entrance door. She didn't hear anything further but silence. Luckily no one came through the kitchen area while she was there.

"What am I thinking? I can't go back in there and look those people in the eye and not tell them, they were just told a bunch of crap! There is something that could have been done!" Manerva thought silently to herself before the outer door to the kitchen opened and in walked several other hospital workers.

They appeared to either be on their lunch or break because both rushed over to get food from the vending machines. Manerva was now sitting with her back to them. She didn't recognize them and they didn't recognize her.

"Do you have any change? This machine just took my money and nothing fall down. They need to fix this. I'm calling this number on this machine and telling them I lost all my money," one of the workers said to the other one.

"Here, take this and calm down. You don't have to go through all those changes just tell the man when he comes in to fill up the machine on our way out in the morning. You know he is usually in here bright and early every wednesday morning. He is so nice and a cutie too. He'll give you your money back or your snack, whichever you want. In fact, I'll tell him you lost it for you," the other worker said with a smile.

"I just bet you will, Miss Thang! Girl I have told you about flirting with every man around, and who told you I needed someone to speak up for me at all," said the first worker. *This was all Manerva could hear as the door closed behind both hospital workers as they left the kitchen area.*

Silence returned in the kitchen area but Manerva could still hear loud crying and talking outside in the waiting room. She quickly got herself together, discarded those two cups of coffee that had become cold. She then got two more cups and poured them with the fresh coffee she had brewed.

"You still here, young lady, I'm glad someone made some fresh coffee," said the same older woman volunteer after she had walked in. She poured herself a cup and sat at the table with Manerva. "You must be pulling an all nighter if you are going to drink both those cups at one time," the volunteer said smiling.

"No, these are for the family members in the waiting room," Manerva said.

The volunteer insisted...

"Give them to me; I'll take them in to them. I had planned on doing it earlier but those pay phones have been ringing off the hooks out there tonight. There were two more families staying over night in there, but one of the other patient's was transferred up on the floors out of ICU and they went with them. All of the other family members left, except the wife, who is in with her husband now during the last visiting hour. She has been living in this waiting room for over eight weeks now. She will not leave. She said she brought her husband into the emergency room for stomach pains and the next thing she knew his appendix went bad. They rushed him to surgery and he's been like a vegetable every since. Poor lady, I make sure I give her pillows ad blankets for the night. She leaves about an hour doing the day and goes to her house and gets clothes. She rushes back here and showers in the lounge on the fourth floor. She says her husband is her life. She also said they had just gotten married five years ago. Listen at me talking, on and on, now I'd better make a fresh pot of coffee, these are old and cold now," the volunteer said while making a fresh pot.

"If you are going to ICU or the recovery room, the elevators are just outside that side door, just down the hall and to your right. That way will get you there faster and sooner. After the last times for visiting hours the front entrance doors outside the waiting room are closed. This allows the families a little privacy. Usually, this time of the night most hospital staff uses the side kitchen doors anyway, so the family members are not alarmed and thinking someone will be bringing them new," the volunteer said warmly.

Manerva took her friendly advice...

"Thanks a lot, for filling me in on everything. I'll just go out the side door. Ma'am, would you make sure you take two cups of fresh hot coffee to the two gentlemen with the lady in the wheelchair," Manerva said as she slowly closed the door thinking about all walking down the hall.

Everything went racing through Manerva's tired and angry body. *"Will Roberta be alright? Why was there no mention of her being pregnant? Maybe, that was just some laboratory gossip! Surely, that would have been a big factor that had to be dealt with and especially in surgery, laser surgery at that! It must be me! I may not have overheard everything too! It's after midnight, and I've got to deal with Dr. Grant in less than six hours. I need to get at least four good hours of sleep or I won't make it," Manerva said as she slowly pushed the button on the elevator to the second floor which led to the hallway to the medical student's dorm room building.*

Manerva didn't know what to do. She didn't like feeling helpless along with everything else. All of the unanswered questions. Another day, feeling powerless. Another day, with Dr. Grant. How much could she take? And why?

"Am I feeling all of this for Roberta or is this about me? I know I'm sick and tired of being and doing and not saying sometimes because of other people. But where is all of this coming from?" Manerva softly asked herself, as she saw a glimpse of her picture sitting on top of her shelf standing smiling with her mother.

"Look at me! I was smiling then, these past few years that I've been in medical school, I really don't smile anymore, not really, I mean, if you didn't know me, you would think I was smiling, but if you really looked deep inside me, you would not see a smile, you would see some of what I saw deep into Roberta's eyes when we first met. But that doesn't make sense. I have never seen Roberta before and I have a family that loves me. All they ever talk about is how proud they are of me! I'm smart! I've got a full scholarship and I'm on my way to becoming what my dad has always wanted me to be, a doctor!" lying there looking up at the high ceilings in this old brownstone building.

She had been as quiet as possible while turning her key to open her dorm door. She had taken a moment and looked around her little dorm room while slowly taking her cloths off and taking a quick shower. There was quiet throughout the bathroom and into the adjacent room on the other side of the bathroom door. She knew either her roommate was sound asleep or she had such a rough day she didn't want to talk about it either also. Nevertheless, Manerva was glad. She didn't want to talk or have to explain anything to anybody. Not now. She really cared about her roommate. She knew Alison would understand. She wanted to talk to her and tell her everything but not tonight. She was just too tired, sleepy and going to bed. She kept asking herself, these same questions over and over as she slowly closed her eyes not even realizing she had fallen fast asleep within minutes.

Chapter Three

I'm Out Of Here!

"Manerva! Manerva! I'm out of here. My first class is at 6:30 am this morning but its way out in East Memphis. Dr. Myers is doing a lecture there this morning on, *How to Become an Effective Doctor No Matter What!* It is the opening of a new Clinic there introducing TeleHealth Medicine. He wants all his med students to attend and participate. He has even chartered a bus to take everybody. The only problem is the bus leaves here at 5:00am. You know, since I'm not from Memphis and have no sense of where any place really is, I figured I'd better make sure I was on time," her roommate said, while talking and shaking Manerva at the same time.

Still talking and shaking...

"Wake up Manerva! Did you hear me? You must have had a long day yesterday, because I went to bed about midnight and you still weren't here. I wasn't sure when you wanted to get up. I haven't heard an alarm go off and I've been up since 3:00am. I had to finish this paper to turn in also," she continued saying.

"Oh my God! Alison, what time is it?" Manerva asked as she struggled to get up.

"It's 4:10 am, and I'm on my way out to grab a bite and catch my bus. Did you hear anything I said?" Alison asked again.

"Yeah, hope all goes well with you and Dr. Myers today and thanks for waking me up! My alarm was set for 3:30am and if it went off I haven't heard a thing," Manerva said.

"I know you are usually up by now and way before me. I haven't heard a thing from this room but you snoring out loud. I just love you Manerva but I'm so glad that adjacent room became available or our friendship would have probably suffer deeply. Got to go, hope you have a good day too," Alison said rushing and smiling out the door.

By now all that could be heard in the room was showering hot water hitting Manerva's entire body. This morning she turned the water up as hot as she could stand it.

"I've got to wake up fast, don't have time to think, got to get out of here too and stop and get something to eat on my way in. I can't chance having another day like yesterday with Dr. Grant!" Manerva said stepping in her pants, getting her lab coat and books and then closing the door behind her.

"Its 4:30 am, I'm good, now I can think, but only about today, I'll think about yesterday later," mumbling to herself walking into a nearby canteen snack area on the other side of the hallway in her brownstone building.

After she drank a cup of coffee, a bottle of juice and ate two sausage biscuit sandwiches plus an apple danish, she knew she was ready to take on Dr. Grant and anything else today!

Rushing down the brownstone's corridor...

Manerva briefly looked outside the corridor's window; she could see all the other med students getting on the chartered bus out in front of the brownstone building. She didn't see Alison, but she knew she was on the bus, *probably the first person sitting right up front behind the bus driver.* She would prepare herself later tonight to hear another one of Alison's bus stories.

You see Alison, was from up north and she loved to ride the bus. She would tell her stories about school buses, tour buses, chartered buses and any other type of bus she had ridden.

"They are like adventures to me. I always meet new people and learn new things. Plus on bus rides I don't get there too fast, and I can always enjoy the scenery," Alison would always say.

Manerva thought this was so fascinating because Alison was from a small suburban area just outside of New York and her family was wealthy. She was an only child and brilliant. She had traveled in some of the most expensive airplanes there was and in first class but she loved her bus adventures the most. She had traveled all around the world with her parents except she had never visited the south. Alison had come to Memphis to mourn the death of Elvis Presley in August of 1977, fell in love with Memphis, told her parents she didn't want to leave, transferred to medical school here and the rest was history.

In fact, her father is part of the network of business developers who donated a lot of money to renovate and remodel the entire downtown and Mississippi Lakefront area. Manerva and Alison became friends the moment they met in orientation. Alison was not your everyday, spoiled rich white girl to Manerva, and Manerva was everything Alison had never imagined a southern black girl to be. They appreciated and learned from one another. Both were tops in their classes.

"Morning Young Lady and you are here on time," Dr. Grant said while looking down at his wristwatch noticing that it was 5:15 am and Manerva was already in an empty room number one of the emergency room sitting in a chair waiting on him when he entered.

"Morning to you also," Manerva responded back with an alertness in her tone that showed sheer confidence.

She was determined to not let him make her feel bad today. She felt good from the start that she was in the room before he had arrived. She knew he had not been there this morning before she had arrived because she had overheard several nurses outside the room talking. They had made comments that it had been noted in the nurses report he had talked to the staff surgeon throughout the night Both nurses had mentioned they were trying to get everything in order before he made his rounds here and before the change of shift. Manerva had too many other things to think about. She was determined to start the day with total control with him. She wanted to know first thing how Roberta was and she knew Dr. Grant knew. She had decided to ask him first thing even if he did not offer any information. And so she did.

"Dr. Grant, do you know how the hit and run patient that was here yesterday evening is doing? They took her to surgery, yesterday evening?" asked Manerva.

"You mean the young female patient named Roberta," Dr. Grant answered.

"Yes, I do believe that was her name," Manerva replied back.

"Unfortunately, she didn't make it through recovery very early this morning. I received a page from Dr. Mahoney about 3:00am this morning. He told me they had to do a code blue on the patient. Dr. Mahoney said she suffered too much internal bleeding and hemorrhaged to death. He had called in Dr. Campling to perform laser surgery because she had encountered some blood reactions. They did the best they could do. Nothing more could be done. That happens, Manerva. Get use to it," Dr. Grant stated.

"Use to it! Nothing more, could be done! I can't believe how cold you said all that! I don't know why I can't believe it from observing you all yesterday. You never once bothered to brief me or talk to me about any of the patients or treatments we observed on yesterday. Had I not asked about this patient you probably never would have told me anything. In fact, I watched you all yesterday, and I noticed you showed little or no compassion toward her," shouted Manerva.

She was angry...

She didn't care who heard her!

"Get control of yourself, young lady, just because there is no one else in this room, gives you no right to speak like that!" he bluntly said back.

"Right! How dare you talk about right! You had no right treating Roberta as if she didn't exist either yesterday! You had no right, letting her just lay on that bed without being treated or you coming back to follow up or monitor her to make sure lab results were in or that your diagnosis had been confirmed! You had no right, to literally threaten me yesterday and tell me not to say anything or question your actions either!" Manerva said without realizing all that was coming out but glad it all did.

"I fault myself, for not following my gut feelings yesterday, it may have saved Roberta! I wonder just how many other patients have you just let die!" Manerva continued talking directly into his face.

"You talk like you knew this Roberta patient, and not like a third year medical student at all! Young lady, I suggest you calm down and be careful of all the insinuations and accusations you are making. In fact, I suggest you leave this room now! I will call your instructor and tell him to re-assign your rotation observation with someone else!" Dr. Grant said, gritting his teeth while trying to keep his composure.

"Do you know what I'd like you to do with what you call insinuations and accusations? And Dr. Grant you don't have to suggest anything to me. I gladly leave this room on my own accord because I want to and not because you suggested anything!" said Manerva with a satisfying sense of control. She then graciously picked up all her belongings and walked pass him and out the door.

As she walked out of the door...

She noticed there was a crowd of people all standing outside in the hallway and near the nurse's station. They seemed to all step back and make an opening for Manerva to walk through. When she did, it felt like all of them were silently cheering her on for saying to Dr. Grant what they each wanted to tell him also. She never looked back, but the coldness she could feel while walking down the hallway let her know, he was still standing by himself in that empty room number one of the emergency room and nobody else wanted to go in.

For that brief moment Manerva felt good, but it didn't last long because deep down there was a sadness that could never be forgotten. She didn't know exactly what she was going to do, but she knew where she had to go. She just hoped it wasn't too late.

As she got off those same front elevators, she saw a different hospital volunteer that was wearing a different red and white candied stripe pinafore over her white dress uniform sitting at the desk by the waiting room. Manerva could hear the pay telephones across from the desk still ringing. Loud crying and talking was coming from within the waiting room but now louder than before. As she looked up to the left side of the room before she walked in she could see another family, more unfamiliar faces but she knew the one sitting on the couch was the women who the older volunteer had told her had brought her husband into the emergency room eight weeks ago. *She just knew it was her.*

She was just sitting there, all made up. Her hair had been combed. She had on a bright yellow outfit with lavender butterflies printed on the upper part of the top. She looked up at me and I looked back at her. She just smiled.

Then, I stopped dead in my tracks before I entered the room to look on the right side of the room. My heart and my focus immediately went back to the women wearing the yellow outfit with the lavender butterflies. Her warm smile let me know, she was thinking while looking over to the other family members.

"At least my husband is still alive!"

I immediately turned around to go through the front doors and go down the side hallway, and as I walked, I was thinking to myself.

"I wonder was Dr. Grant, the staff intern in the emergency department the day she brought her husband in." It didn't matter.

In fact at that moment nothing else mattered...

As I took that same journey back through the door from the kitchen area of the waiting room and into the hallway I walled down that lonely hall. I hadn't noticed before but as I crossed over to the recovery room area into the step down unit there were pictures on both sides of the walls. This unit was one of the newly built and renovated wings of the hospital. Before it was built this area was part of the lobby area of the main hospital. I managed to somehow look up at the pictures on the same right side that I was walking pass. They were in beautiful gold looking frames. A quick thought rushed through my mind at that very moment as I noticed those pictures.

"Bates was absolutely right! Here is the proof! As I looked closer I could see. I took another moment out to further confirm my suspicions and there they were bottom right was Dr. Henry T. Grant Sr. and top left was the late Mitchell D. Grant. It didn't take a rocket scientist to figure it out," Manerva thought to herself in a moment of sadness.

I then braced myself...

Then I slowly walked in the recovery room, and there she was. They had moved her into this large room now. She didn't recognize me, she couldn't recognize me. Her eyes were closed, her hair was all messed up, all sort of gels and tubes were on her body; but the one thing that stood out the most was her stomach; it had blown up and looked like a nine month old pregnant woman. Here again, it seemed like yesterday, when we both met for the first time. We were not properly introduced, but somehow we managed to meet, we communicated, maybe not with a lot of conversation, but somehow we understood one another, we both felt each other," said Manerva while walking over closer to her bed.

Several hospital workers came to the door and turned back around, when they saw Manerva standing next to Roberta. They seemed as though they had just changed shifts, but even they wanted to give Roberta the respect she deserved with her visitor. They knew their job could wait.

So standing again, close to her bed and looking up at the recovery room clock this time seeing that it was now 7:15 am. Less than twenty fours since we had both met and both looking into each other eyes. Now when I look there is no looking back.

Manerva noticed all the equipment on the different carts, and with all of the strength she could whisper said softly.

"Roberta, I'm sorry. I hope one day you will forgive me. I hope

you understand and know how much I wanted to do the right thing. It seems now after the fact that I needed you also at the same time you needed me. I needed your strength and courage Roberta. Please forgive me. Somehow I know this is about you and not me. I let you down. You are not here to defend yourself anymore. As tears continued to softly fall from both Manerva's light brown eyes, she continued talking.

"I needed you to come into my life to let me see myself. I don't know all the details of everything that has happened to you, my friend, but just be at peace. Now your eyes are closed from any more pain. Just know, I can't imagine all of what happened to you on yesterday or even your life before, but know the love you leave showed through your family last night and now. They were here, they are still here, and they will forever be with you in your heart. I'll just say so long for now my friend, because I'm sure we will meet again. Just know you have changed my life and I will forever be grateful."

Manerva slowly grabbed the end of the sheet at the foot of her bed and brought it up to cover her body. As she slowly walked out and looked back she saw Roberta, lying there one last time just sleeping, peacefully, *with her deep dark brown eyes closed but with a warm subtle smile in an empty room.*

"Are you a member of the family, Doctor?" the nursing assistant asked Manerva as she passed her going into Roberta's room.

"Just a close friend," Manerva said softly.

"I was just told some more of the family members want to come up and visit her before they come in and move her body. Usually they would have had everything moved and cleaned up in here by now, but I overheard everybody talking about the accident and how everything happened so fast. They say they haven't even contacted all of her family members yet. Sad, someone would just run her over like that, and leave her to die. Only a monster could do that! They say she went to nursing school here! Just a shame! She was so young, and had her whole life ahead of her! Let me hurry up, they pulled me from on the other end to get things together in here because some of her family members are coming in from the waiting room. That's why I thought you were from her family," the nursing assistant told Manerva.

"It was on the 10 o'clock news last night, I missed it. I was off yesterday but just didn't get a chance to watch the TV much yesterday. Everybody was talking about it in the locker room this morning. They say there were reporters here today, asking questions. My supervisor told us in a meeting this morning to just do our jobs and try not to talk to anyone. Must be a big stink. Lord knows, I need my job," the other nursing assistant said to the other while talking aloud and finishing up brushing Roberta's hair.

Manerva and both of the nursing assistants walked out of Roberta's room only moments before they each turned slightly and looked back down the hallway, as they both heard loud screams and crying coming from within her room.

"How could they just let my baby die like this!" shouted a loud female voice from within the room. Somebody know something, it just don't make sense! No, I'm not going to be quiet! Roberta! Roberta! Wake up baby, its mama! Talk to me! You open your eyes up! Open them, I say!" she kept screaming out before the man put his arms around her and helped her to a chair.

Manerva could see the staff all standing back, there was only one other patient's room across the hall that they went over and closed that room's door, as if it would prevent them from hearing everything that was going on in Roberta's room. Three of Roberta's family member's had stepped out of the room as if they were trying to get some air and compose themselves. The older man went back in; he didn't see or recognize Manerva standing down the hallway by the rollaway bed standing against the wall. But Manerva recognized him,

"He wanted the cup of black coffee last night. I wonder are you Roberta's father?" She continued to think to herself aloud. I bet the lady screaming that they are trying to calm down in the room is Roberta's mom and the older blind lady in the wheelchair is Roberta's grandmother on her father's side. That's why the older man is now bent down on his knees with his head placed on the blind lady's lap while she is just rubbing the top of his bald

head with her right hand. She seemed to have had a stroke and paralyzed on her left side. Everything seemed to calm down for a while. They were still in Roberta's room but there were no more loud screams or cries, only sadness," thought Manerva.

Just then...

Manerva quickly became startled; she listened carefully while staying out of sight because she knew she recognized the voice.

"But where is he, I hope he didn't see me. So what if he did. I'm not answering to him any longer. You may have power with the staff here because of your father, but not me!" Manerva thought to herself.

There was some type of manager's office on the other side of the wall that she was standing by. She had noticed it earlier when she got off the front elevators. She was behind now where the service elevators were. She didn't know who else was in that room, but she was certain one of the people was Dr. Grant. She could hear his voice a mile away, even with her eyes closed. A quick flash came to mind.

"I know Roberta heard him too, it didn't matter if she couldn't speak, she heard with her eyes, she heard even if her eyes were closed," said Manerva.

No Manerva was just where she needed to be, she didn't need to try to get any closer or move anywhere else. She had to just stop, think, and follow her gut feeling.

"She's in the room on the left; they paged earlier and want us to take the body to the basement first. The family is requesting that an autopsy be done immediately," one of the transport workers said to the other one, as they pushed the transport bed off the service elevator down the hallway.

"Last autopsy, I heard about at this hospital was when they did it on *The King* and boy do I remember all that! I was even working the night he came in through the service elevators down by the emergency room near the helicopter drop off. He walked into the hospital that night and had on a black trench coat. He had all his body guards around him," " the older transport worker said bragging to the younger transport worker as he picked up the papers with his instructions in his hand pushing the bed pass Manerva.

The elevator door opened and Manerva stepped inside. There was too much going on and she didn't need to be seen anymore. She had been privileged to know all she needed to know. She knew what she needed to do was help sort things out to help find some answers. She had to think about what to do next. Roberta's case surely had marked a crossroad in her career and maybe in her life.

At this very moment...

She knew she had her work cut out. The one other sure thing Manerva now knew was that she had absolutely no idea what she was going to do next. Yesterday about the same time of day, being a third year medical school student, being tops in her class, being on a full scholarship and, pleasing her family all meant something and seemed so very important. She just couldn't understand how one case that happened less than twenty fours ago had changed all that. Walking and thinking, walking and thinking, now as she turned the lock, she gently pushed the door back, and looked around her dorm room.

"I'll set this alarm for exactly one hour, then it will be 9:00am, I'll get back up and start my day!" Manerva said quietly lying back and just closing her eyes.

Chapter Four

Timing Is Everything!
Chicago, Illinois, 1992

It had been almost fifteen years exactly...

Except instead of a hot, humid day, Manerva woke up to an almost windy, chilling freeze outside. Even though she was now thirty six years old, she often thought about that case.

"A good hot cup of tea sounds so good."

"The only problem is I've got to get up out of bed to make it. Where are my slippers? I love to look at these beautiful old hardwood floors but not walking on them in cold weather like this at seven o'clock in the morning," she said while still reaching on the side of her bed.

Ring! Ring! Ring! From her telephone...

"Okay, I'm trying to get to you as fast as I can," said Manerva while placing the receiver to her right ear.

"Good Morning, rise and shine," came from the voice on the other end of the receiver.

"Good Morning Deanna," drowsily said by Manerva.

"Better get an early start, have you looked out your window yet?" Deanna asked.

"No, why?"

"Well, I know you get that lake effect snow, on top of what we get, and we got six inches of snow already! I just looked at the news and they said this slipped up on everybody. You know Chicago's weathermen are usually always right, but they didn't catch this one. They said the salt trucks were just getting out there. You know morning rush hour is going to be unreal, especially for me" Deanna said.

"Boy, that's all I needed to hear, to get me up and fast," said Manerva.

"Change of plans, I'll just leave my car parked, and catch a cab. That's one of the reason's I love living in Chicago, they have the best transit system around. You can go all over the city and not move your car. Well enough of us talking, I've got to get things together. You and your family still excited about your dad's big night in three days?" Manerva asked.

"Yeah, you know my dad, in fact, he was the one who called me and told me about the snow. You will probably see him there, he said he got there at 4:00am to prepare for an important client meeting this morning," said Deanna.

It was times like these when Manerva was able to not only attend meetings but voice her opinions as well, that she would think about her years in med school back in Memphis, and smile and be glad she had decided to leave. She was so glad it was her decision.

"No time for tea today, got to get ready," said Manerva. As she got in the shower and was dressing she thought back on that day.

That hot, humid morning...

She had just gone back to her room to think about what she was going to do. That morning she was only able to rest for fifteen minutes, before her pager went off.

"I recognize that telephone number, it's from the Dean of Students office," Manerva had said. She immediately, answered her page, and was told when she called,

"Manerva, you need to come to the Dean's Office at once. Make sure you have your student ID card, all of your lab coats

and books," the secretary said, before hanging up the telephone not letting Manerva ask or say anything.

So she did, feeling in her heart, what would happen next. Manerva, remembering back that day she walked the opposite way down the hallway. When she arrived at the Dean of Student's door, the secretary gave her a nod, letting her know she was to go straight in. As she had expected Dr. Grant was already sitting in one of the two chairs that was across the other side of the large oak desk.

"Good Morning, Manerva, would you please have a sit. Let me get right to the point. Dr. Grant has given me a very disturbing report regarding your irrational behavior toward him within a patient's room, in fact, room number one in the emergency department. Along with his report, he has a list of five other hospital workers who said they witnessed your behavior. Might I add Ms. Jones, this type of behavior is unacceptable and will not be tolerated under any circumstances. I'd like for you to look over this report, and I'd like to hear your comment at once, Ms. Jones," he had said as candidly as possible.

I remember, standing up, and not reaching out at all to get the report he was trying to give me. I took off my lab coat, and placed it on his large oak desk, along with the bag of extra lab coats, my student ID badge, and all my books. I remember, stepping away from the chair I had sat down in and saying as I was leaving his office.

"I pray that both of you have a good day, this is not for me!" smiling as I left the room.

"If you leave Ms. Jones, you will not be able to return and you loose all of your remainder scholarship money," said Dr. Grant.

Manerva looked at Dr. Grant, and said,

"Do you really want me to tell you what you can do with the scholarship money? I don't think so! I pity you Dr. Grant!"

Pushing back the shower door...

Manerva stepped out and reached for the towel. Even on this cold, windy Chicago day, and even with the hard wood floors, Manerva still smiled with pride as she looked into her own eyes in her big full mirror that covered the entire side of her bathroom wall. She was OK, she had gotten pass all that and gone on with her life. Her focus now was to concentrate on a big event happening in three days.

"In a lot of way's I guess there are a lot of similarities because I will again be in the midst of the hospital and medical school staff members but the big difference now is that I feel empowered," Manerva thought silently while stepping into a nice navy blue designer pant suit and matching shoes.

Putting finishing touches on make up and all, Manerva then grabbed her little black cart, coat and boots out of her front closet before she headed out of her front door. This was one of the things she enjoyed best by living in her prominent Chicago lakefront area. It didn't matter what the weather was like. The city kept her street clean and the building engineer made sure the outside grounds to her condominium were always kept clean. Public transportation was great. She could just leave her car parked in her garage and take either a cab, the CTA or the L-train from her street. Cabs circled her block almost every ten minutes so there was never a need to call for one. She could even call and the cab driver would buzz her intercom button in her lobby waiting and would push her little black cart out for her.

Yes, she just smiled, as she stepped inside the cab, ready to start her day. A big contrast from the Manerva fifteen years ago back in Memphis. Just as she knew it would be, the streets had been salted and cleared of snow. Even in rush hour traffic, driving along Lake Michigan was breath taking. Manerva, almost always would mentally be prepared by taking her laptop from within her little black cart and make sure she had all of her power point presentations in order before she arrived at her office or a morning briefing meeting.

No time to think about that day, fifteen years ago, because today, Manerva could actually thank that day. It was really, that day that helped her make her decision and she had never regretted it. That day a lot of things went through her mind, but she was glad she had left and had gone on with her life.

The first couple of years after she had left Memphis were really hard. She had never mentioned to anyone that Bates had told her he overheard a couple of med techs in the lab saying her urine test showed she was pregnant, not even Alison. Things had happened so fast, and she knew whatever had happened there was no record or no mention of it. Even though the feeling never left Manerva, she had decided to just let Roberta's family accept her death as best they could. Manerva knew whatever had happened had been wiped away and done away with just as quickly as she had been.

She had thought long and hard that day fifteen years ago and within fifteen short minutes of analyzing and looking at the big picture Manerva remembered seeing all the pictures of the board of trustees hanging on the hospital walls and all of what had happened and about the things Bates had told her. She knew she could put up a fight but she wouldn't win that battle. Her thoughts were further confirmed when the Dean of Students had presented her with a report with five witnesses. It all became reality to Manerva then because how could there have been witnesses when the door was closed and the room was completely empty with no patient. She had glanced the report and they saw each witness claimed they were all inside the room at the time observing along with me while Dr. Grant was performing his diagnosis on the patient. How could she have fought all that? Would she have ever won? Other than her family, church and one or two close friends including Alison, know body would ever know she had been a medical student. All that had happened was just a feeling for Manerva.

Several times she had filled out applications when she first moved to Chicago just to see and list her medical school experience as a reference, only to have everyone returned that nothing could be verified because each response was there was no record. It was as though she started her life over. It wasn't easy, but through the grace of God, determination, and the friends she had met through Alison she had endured. She not only endured she had made a very noteworthy life for herself. Deep down in her memories she would never forget anything and she felt that Saturday's banquet was for her as well. She had personally invited all of the people in her life that meant something to her and that she wanted to thank.

Manerva was happy with her career...

Being the only black female and the youngest, for the past five years serving as a legal consultant for NorthCentral Hospital. She also shared a small law practice with two other attorneys in the downtown Chicago area. This was a dream come true for Manerva. She had worked hard, gotten accepted into law school. At first she went part time and had a lot of evening classes. She was happy because this is what she really wanted to do. She was very proud of herself. Her family was proud of her also. She had worked so hard the past fifteen years, most of the time holding down three to four jobs at a time.

Shortly, after that day in Memphis fifteen years ago, she decided to leave Memphis and move to Chicago. She felt there were more opportunities in Chicago that she could take advantage of. She left Memphis on a mission. She no longer had a scholarship, but she could get loans, and she worked odd jobs to pay her tuition. She only knew she wanted to be involved in that part of the system that made some legal decisions; that part of the system that made people accountable for theirs actions. She wanted to be able to have a voice and know it would be heard. Things were very different now.

She was excited about attending the banquet on Saturday. It would be honoring the father of one of her best friend: everyone including Manerva will be commending Dr. Wayne T. Sumner on his publication of *PRE AND POST CARDIAC SURGERY RESEARCH-UPDATES*, but silently Manerva will be celebrating and thanking God, for her accomplishments. The years had been hard ones, but they had been good to her.

Even though it seemed that she had just up and left that almost haunting situation with Roberta, she would never forget. Through the years, she would often think of those eyes, and they still were as vivid each time as they were the first. When she left Memphis, she would visit her family on occasion usually doing the holidays and since they knew nothing about Roberta, she became Manerva's private memory. It was already hard enough on her family to accept the idea that she was no longer in medical school and was living over six hundred miles away.

There had been many times Manerva wanted to talk about it especially with her family.

"I have a cousin who works in one of those nearby hospitals as a receptionist; I could get her to check or snoop around and tell me about any rumors on Dr. Grant," she would often think about.

"No one would understand why I was that concerned about someone, I had never met before?"

"They already thought it was weird I left medical school anyway!"

"No one really said it, but I could feel it, so many times."

"I knew they loved me and could never understand. Whatever happened to Roberta or how it affected Manerva was too deep to talk about.

So many times, she wanted to go back and talk to her parents. She wanted to find out was there any truth to the rumors about her being pregnant? No matter how many times, she thought about Roberta and all these unanswered questions, she would get the same answer.

"What good would it do? She would only open up Pandora's Box in a sense. She had no proof. She was in no position to do anything even if she had found out anything. She had to think about herself and go on with her own life. She had to also think about how what she would say affect Roberta's family and even her own family. Manerva knew down deep, the only proof she had was her feelings.

And so, knowing all of that was the one thing she knew she would never forget or let go of.

With a smile now instead of the anger...

At some point Saturday night at the banquet, she knew she would make a silent toast to her unknown friend with the *dark brown eyes (Roberta)* who helped change her life. Her life now, fifteen years later, had meaning and purpose. She had worked hard, and she was in a position finally, that her voice was heard. At this point in her life it felt good to somehow, speak up and be recognized by her merit of hard work. She knew deep down no matter what, that Roberta did understand because she was a major driving force for her at that crossroad in her life.

She would forever be grateful to her roommate, Alison, and what she had done also. *She always felt Alison was one of her little guardian angel.* Smiling, now sitting back as the cab driver slowly drove in the rush hour traffic bumper to bumper and looking out over a powdered frozen Lake Michigan, Manerva continued reminiscing.

"Manerva, don't be stubborn, take this name, address and phone number and promise me you will call them, once your bus gets into the terminal. I have already told them to expect your call. They are my god parents and they own property and several apartment buildings throughout all of Chicago. They also have a lot of professional networking connections. He is a retired lawyer and she is a retired doctor. They never had any children that's why they love me so. They will be there for you. Let them," Alison had pleaded with Manerva.

"Manerva, what has happened here at school is just between us. No one else ever needs to know. All I have told my godparents are is you are my friend, we met in medical school, and you will be moving to Chicago and will need a place to stay. I told them you were like a sister to me, and that's all they need to know," Alison said as we both hugged and cried and said our good byes over and over.

She had been a real friend throughout my stay at medical school. She knew I would never take money from her and she knew I didn't know anyone in Chicago but was determined to make it. I often smile thinking, how you never know how things will turn out. In fact, I am so excited that in three days, I'll see my friend ago; I haven't seen her since her wedding two years ago. I finally, got a chance to meet her parents, and it wasn't at all like the movie, *Guess Who Is Coming To Dinner.*

"I say that not only because of me being her maid of honor in her wedding, but because the groom was Bates the lab tech. My dad just really got a laugh at all that and he still jokes about it now," Manerva thought smiling as the cab driver pulled up in front of her law practice front door.

"Thanks, this is for you, keep the change and have a beautiful day," Manerva told the cabdriver.

As Manerva walked into the large Chicago historic building looking as if it was designed by Frank Lloyd Wright himself, she looked around the lobby. Traffic was just as usual. People were walking in and out of the revolving glass door, some went to the right to the restaurant, some were standing waiting on the elevators, and some were just sitting inside the lobby just reading or relaxing while the fireplace was burning. The Sears Tower building was just a couple of blocks over.

"Morning, Manerva, I left a file in your In-Box this morning. I'd like for you to review it and tell me what you think before I sign it," an older male voice said coming up from behind her while she was waiting on the elevator.

She immediately turned around because she recognized the voice...

"Good morning, Dr. Sumner, I'll look it over first then," Manerva said back.

"I just finished talking to Deanna, and she told me you were on your way in. She says, I'm an over protective dad still calling to check up on her. She's probably right, but this morning, I just wanted her to know about the snow, because it was a surprise to everyone. Anyway, I just came down to sit down and relax and eat something, because I've been up in my office working since about 4:00am. Everybody laughs at me, but they make the best breakfast ever. When I don't eat at home, this is the next best thing. I've got two very important clients meeting me in less than an hour," Dr. Sumner said.

"Don't worry Dr. Sumner, you are just being a dad, mine does me the same way and he is over six hundred miles away. I'll go straight up and review your file. It will be in your In-box with all my comments, when you return," Manerva said as the elevator door opened.

It didn't matter to Manerva that as she walked into their law practice, her office was one of the smallest offices in the suite. It was large enough for her. She had been Dr. Sumner's apprentice six years ago, and he had always told her how much he admired her hard work. He was a man of his word because when his other partner moved away, he immediately gave her a call and made her an offer that she could not refuse. He had taken a big chance on her and she would not let him down.

As she passed the reception area, she looked and noticed there were several files in her In-Box. She didn't have any appointments scheduled until later, so she spoke to the receptionist, got her files, and went into her office.

The red light on her desk phone was blinking to show she had messages waiting. Since she was in earlier than she had originally planned to be and since her first priority was to review Dr. Sumner's file. She said reasoning with herself.

"I'll check all my phone and email messages after I finish reviewing this file."

She knew if there were any emergencies, she would have been contacted through her cellular phone, pager or 2-way radio. So she turned her radio on down very low on her very favorite classical music station and started reviewing Dr. Sumner's file. This case was involving a matter with a discrimination matter involving an employee and his supervisor, the employee had contacted union representatives, and the company wanted Dr. Sumner to represent them. Manerva gave the review her undivided attention, placing all of her comments in Dr. Sumner's file.

She knew he would understand everything she wrote. When it came to business she and Dr. Sumner thought very much alike. She too was very familiar with how Dr. Sumner felt about several of the issues that were listed. She had worked with him on many similar cases in the past. She realized and appreciated that she was being trained by one of Chicago's finest. Dr. Sumner was a lawyer and a doctor. He primarily focused now in handling a lot of major labor dispute cases, while doing a lot of medical research. She had just finished assisting him on a lot of State and medical findings with the Joint Commission. Manerva had never worked with or seen anyone so dedicated to their work. Dr. Sumner was her mentor. She felt honored that he respected and admired her and her opinions so. There was another attorney that was a senior partner in the law firm as well. He was much older than Manerva and who had been practicing law almost as long as Dr. Sumner. One of the things Manerva had noticed was how much Dr. Sumner asked her advice rather than the other attorney. They were old friends. They belonged to a lot of the same clubs and played a lot of golf together but when it really came to business, it appeared to Manerva that for what ever the reason was Dr. Sumner really valued how she thought and she liked that.

After she finished her review...

She went to leave them so he would have them once he finished eating. She noticed all of Dr Sumner's other files and materials were still there, which indicated he had not come back up or he would have taken all from his In-Box. Manerva slipped her review file under his door. She then went back into her office and closed the door; she picked up her desk telephone receiver, and typed in her code to retrieve all of her incoming messages. She had a total of five. Two were business and three were from Kenneth. *Kenneth was Manerva's personal business. Manerva wrote down the messages regarding her two business calls, she would take care of them later.*

Chapter Five

Hearts Hardened!

As Manerva started to listen to her three calls from Kenneth she reached over and changed the radio station from classical to her favorite *dusties* as the D J called them. Playing at that very moment was an old Marvin Gaye tune; *Heaven must have sent you from Above*. As she listened to Kenneth voice, she was softly humming and singing the words along with the record. This song brought back old memories and she hoped, no one would knock or call at that very moment because she didn't want to be disturbed. Manerva loved excitement and she loved people. Now, that she was successful in her career, she spent a lot more time concentrating on her personal life. She had been involved in a number of relationships over the years, even before she had left Memphis. Some she was proud of and some she was not.

She had her moments just as any other hard working; ambitious female would desiring to have that special man in her life. She wanted to love and to really be loved. Even though she was happy in her career, she realized there were missing pieces to her total puzzle of happiness.

As far back as Manerva, as she could remember she could hear people saying all her life.

"You are such a good person" or

"You have such a good heart."

Deep down, she knew they were right, and even though she had sacrificed a great deal of her life toward her family and her career. She still had managed to find time to meet people and enjoy herself. With all her intellect and knowledge, she couldn't understand why she kept becoming involved in bad relationships.

Manerva always knew she was blessed. She always wanted to do the right thing. And when she didn't, she always felt bad. She always wanted to share her happiness with the people she became involved with. To some, this could have been perceived as a sign of weakness, but to Manerva, this was one of her greatest strengths. She always looked for the good in people, realizing their faults, just as her own, but not concentrating on them. This was not a preconceived agenda that she purposely set out to have. The only thing she wanted from them was for them to share in her happiness. She knew, and believed in her heart that if they could do this—they really loved her.

But over the years and through countless encounters, she found this not to be the case. So, Manerva's heart started to harden; she became very cautious, and it became harder for her to trust. She didn't like being this way, because it really wasn't her. But she felt she had to protect herself from being hurt. Manerva knew deep down she was at another crossroad, this time with her own personal life. She had become more like this within the past five years. She played Kenneth's messages back a couple of times.

"Kenneth, are you telling me the truth about what I mean to you? You sure sound good to me! When I close my eyes, and hear your voice I can feel your arms around me," She said in a soft sweet whisper.

Just then, there was a sudden knock at her door...

Causing her to quickly snap out of her trance.

"Yes," said Manerva.

"Ms. Jones, is it okay if I go next door to see if I can help with their fax machine, today is their receptionist first day on the job, and she came in to ask me about it, she seemed a nervous wreck, and I remember I've been there? I can forward all calls into our answering service until I return. I should only be a few minutes," the receptionist explained.

"Of course go help; I don't have any appointments this morning, just transfer the calls to me, and I'll watch out front until you return," said Manerva.

"Thank You Ms. Jones, said the receptionist, she's my friend's daughter, and I don't want her to get fired her first day. I'll be right back," said the receptionist.

Manerva went back to her desk and kept her door open. She could see the front door of the reception area if she moved her chair over to the left a bit. She could also hear the door chime each time it opened if she left her door open.

Her day had started now...

She turned her radio off, took her daytimer planner out and took her ink pen out. *She would think more about her personal life later.*

About ten minutes, later the receptionist returned.

"Thanks again, Ms. Jones, we got it all taken care of, they had delivered the wrong type of fax film for their fax machine and there was no instruction manual, I've worked with that type before, so I was familiar with it. I'll work through my break to make up for the time," said the receptionist.

"No, you will not! It was no problem at all. It was actually my pleasure, considering all the extra things you do for each of us and around the office. Donna, these two gentlemen are clients of Dr. Sumner. Will you escort, both of them to the large conference room, and offer them some coffee and donuts; he'll be with them shortly? Would you also start the video which gives an overview of our law firm and some things they may look forward to? I'll let Dr. Sumner know his clients are waiting in the large conference room. He is in his office looking over the files and proposal I just gave him earlier.

The receptionist greeted both gentlemen and walked them down the hallway and to the left into the large conference room. After they were seated she placed a tray of bagels with cream cheese and an assortment of donuts on the large oval shaped conference table. "Coffee, juice or tea," she asked. One of the men answered.

"Coffee, black for me, thank you." The other gentleman quickly answered also.

"Juice for me, thanks."

As they both sat eating and waiting, Dr. Sumner looked over his files and seemed pleased. "Thanks, Manerva, I agree with all your comments, I was thinking the same thing, I just wanted a second opinion, since I've done business with both of these gentlemen before and this is a tough case," he said sticking his head in her door as he passed walking toward the conference room.

As she looked at her schedule, she had a special meeting at NorthCentral Hospital today at four o'clock with their advisory board, where she had been invited to attend to discuss a malpractice lawsuit involving an unnecessary surgery performed resulting in the death of a patient. There would be a formal meeting with the entire review board on Monday, but today Manerva wanted to gather as much information as possible.

It just so happened that the medical examiner for NorthCentral Hospital was her neighbor and friend, Dr. Rhonda Parks. She had been to several cook outs Dr. Rhonda Parks and her husband had. Her husband Dr. Vernon Parks loved to cook. He had retired from the medical profession and owned several restaurants in the downtown area. For the past three years he had his three restaurants set up at the *Taste of Chicago*. He would brag for days about his special barbeque sauce. One year he had baskets sent to everyone in our apartment building for the Fourth of July, filled with cooked barbecue ribs and the fixings along with his special sauce. That was his passion and it was good. Manerva often told Rhonda what a nice couple they made.

"You are the blessed one to have a man that absolutely loves you, and cooks for you."

Rhonda usually would respond back with, "I know, because you know I can't cook, and after I come home from work, cooking is the farthest thing on my mind. He is the only person; I know that can easily get my mind off of work and into him, just like that. I just love that man. And it doesn't seem like we've been married for eighteen years!"

One of the two business messages I had received earlier was from Dr. Parks saying she had to be in the building later today and wanted to stop by my office about one o'clock to have a briefing about her report findings and give me some feedback before the meeting at four o'clock today. The other message is a reminder about my budget meeting next week that I'll take care of later," Manerva thought to herself.

She had fallen for Kenneth, more than she had wanted to. She had wanted to call him back now, but his other message was that he was on his way out of town to a business conference in New York. He wasn't exactly sure what time he would be back because of weather delays.

"I'll call you, baby, first chance I get," he said, as she played the message back and smiled thinking about the other night. While sitting and smiling, her phone rang again and she picked up, knowing it was Deanna this time thanks to caller ID.

"One of the things I really like about Kenneth is how he courts me. I mean the old fashioned courting, the way my dad courted my mom Deanna. This man is really messing me up! He really wines and dines me and treats me like I want to be treated."

"You deserve it," Deanna said back.

"I know, but with my past track record with relationships lately, I'm too scared to believe it could be real. The other night was fantastic though, we went to that new Broadway play showing at the Chicago Theater and afterwards he took me to dinner over looking Lake Michigan. It was breathtaking sitting at our table while the floor actually revolved while we were sitting there. All you could see was different sceneries over looking the skyline, looking into this sexy man's face. And he looked back just as inviting. It didn't make things any better when he told me his dad had brought his mom here on one of their anniversaries. He was even a perfect gentleman afterwards, walking me to my door, and kissing me goodnight," said Manerva.

"I like that he took the initiative whether it was true or not to tell me we better call it a night, because if it had gone any further he probably wouldn't want to leave or stop. This messed me up, because I knew this man was into me. And Deanna, I was into him too! We both felt it and we both knew to slow it down. We are still trying to get to know each other. We've known each other less than a month. We both just got out of bad relationships. It's not easy but we both know we need to slow it on down! My prior engagement you know was nothing but a joke and his divorce had just become final two months became we met. We both are still so vulnerable and don't want to be on the rebound of one another too quick.

And when he left things didn't get any better, because he had stirred up every hormone I had in me and either he was faking it or he's too good, because later at about two thirty in the morning I was awakened by a gentle ringing of my telephone. When I realized I was not dreaming, I picked it up on the third ring knowing it was him from my caller ID. He doesn't say much, but his voice, his tone, his body! Do you really know what I mean Deanna?" asked Manerva.

"You know I definitely do Manerva but just enjoy him, and take it slow. Remember we both know who really has your heart, whether you ever admit how much you love Michael or not. We both know your heart will never be satisfied to settle, don't make the mistake I made with Roman. If nothing else learn from my mistake. Take some of your own advice you always gave me to just listen to the realness of your own heart. We'll talk later, I've got to go!" Deanna said before they both hung up sounding like two teenagers.

Kenneth was definitely someone worth getting to know better…

Unlike Manerva's previous engagement, she actually liked Kenneth. She liked what he stood for. Dr. Kenneth H. Donavon, Ph.D. in history, and Master of science in environmental engineering; thirty seven years old, Vice-President of Academic Affairs at South Chicago State University and Regional Music Director of the Southwest Division. In his spare time he played jazz and blues, and was also the music director at his church. It wasn't easy for Manerva to stay focused when she closed her eyes and thought about this six foot, smooth dark skinned man, with a neatly trimmed beard and the best smile in town.

"*When I hear his voice I can still feel him wrapping his long arms around my body and caressing me as we danced and enjoyed one another almost all night. He even had some steppin moves that he pulled her into his arms and held on tight. Yes, this man is smooth,*" Manerva though to herself.

They hadn't gone out a lot, because both of them had very busy schedules but when they went out, it was like heaven. He had one daughter, six years old who he adored. He talked of wanting to spend more time with her. Both Manerva and Kenneth needed more time and space to heal from the hurt of their prior bad relationships. Manerva knew patience was a virtue she was working desperately at having with her personal relationships. In her professional career, it was no problem and it was one of her most cherished strengths. Now with everything else that would be happening at the Banquet in three days, she would be faced with another turning point. This time she felt it would be dealing with her personal relationships. She had tried to be as honest with herself as possible. How would she have known when she started helping with all the planning for this event she was going to meet Kenneth? How was she to know the last man she had ever truly loved would end up being Congressman and the surprise guest speaker at the award Banquet in three days?

Deanna had called right back...

To let her know she had checked over the guest list and Congressman Michael C. Glenn had confirmed his rsvp. Dr. Sumner, had asked Congressman Glenn to be the guest speaker. Dr. Sumner had always admired Michael. He had wanted to surprise both Deanna and Manerva. He had instructed the event planner to just place on the program *guest speaker* with no name beside it. Both Deanna and Manerva just put two and two together and figured out Michael was the guest speaker. They were pleased for that and decided not to spoil Dr. Sumner's surprise by letting him know, they knew.

Dr. Sumner had formed a special bond with Michael almost from the very first day he had stopped in at the coffee house and saw the three of them studying together nine years ago. Michael had almost become like the son he had loss. You just knew by being around the two of them, how much alike they really were. One young, one old. They had all often read about Michael's accomplishments, but neither had seen Michael since the primary election in November five years ago.

On a more personal note they hadn't seen each other since the dinner at the Sumner's home in March of that same year five years ago. No one was surprised when they picked up the newspapers and heard on the radio that Michael was running for Mayor of Chicago. He had pulled together a campaign almost single handedly. Both Deanna and Manerva always suspected that Dr. Sumner had a lot to do with helping him with that campaign? We both just stayed out of his way when it came to Michael, his politics and all of his networking connections. We weren't surprised the day Michael loss. Dr. Sumner took it well also and had a press conference set up announcing his total support for the Democratic Party. The look in his eye that day was as though he was glad Michael didn't win.

All Dr. Sumner would say was, "It wasn't Michael's time; Chicago wasn't ready for a black Mayor." He would even tell us stories of how Chicago had treated Dr. King when he came. Over dinner Michael would share stories of the politics he experienced back in Memphis. He'd tell how his father had taken him to see Dr. King when he was in Memphis with the Sanitation Strike. Dr. Sumner especially liked hearing Michael's stories and mine, especially when I would tell how my father was a preacher and some of the things our family had to endure growing up from the south. After Michael and I heard and saw Dr. and Mrs. Sumner, we both understood where Deanna got her strong will from.

We all found each other fascinating...

We had each met nine years ago on North Central's campus. Michael and Manerva were in law-school, and Deanna was in med-school. Manerva and Deanna would occasionally meet up every chance they could in a nearby coffee house between classes. One cold snowy day, Deanna and Manerva had both looked up almost at the same time, looking into the eyes of the best looking black man they had seen in a very long time. That was rare because other than Manerva there were very few blacks on campus period. They tried to keep a straight face, but it was almost impossible. After a short while, this young man came over and introduced himself, making a play and being a gentleman at the same time.

"Two of Chicago's finest ladies on campus, Hi my name is Michael, may I join you?" he said very politely.

"Of course, I'm Manerva"

"And, my name is Deanna," they each said, with their mouths still wide open.

"I've seen both of you around campus a few times, you live on campus?" he asked."

"I do, I'm a second year medical student," said Deanna.

"I live off campus about five miles away," said Manerva.

"I've seen you in some of my political science lectures," Michael said.

"Someday, I hope to be the next Mayor of Chicago, so I'm trying to learn all I can about the politics here, because I'm from a small town just outside of Memphis, TN," Michael said.

Just then, both ladies looked at each other, as if to see who would speak next. Then Deanna, being the ever ready match maker said, "Manerva is from Memphis, also!"

"Get out of here! Then home girl, we've got to get together and talk! How about this weekend, that is after I take both you ladies out. I hear a live comedy show will be at the Park West, how about it?" asked Michael.

"OK for me, each said as he got up as quickly as he had come.

"Nice meeting, both of you ladies, I have another lecture in fifteen minutes and I don't want to be late. I'm sure I'll see both of you around before the weekend, take care."

"Me too," said Manerva, quickly getting up and getting her things.

"My next lab is not for another hour, said Deanna, so I'll see you two later, I'm going to sit here for a while and go over my notes."

Deanna looked out the coffee shop's window as she sat at her favorite table and ordered another cup of cappuccino and watched Michael and Deanna walk around the corner back toward the campus. NorthCentral was one of Chicago's biggest and best not only because of its great location but because it was one of the few places ever that had a School of Medicine and School of Law all under one roof. It was so large that it took up the entire two blocks. The Hospital was just across the street and around the corner were a number of law offices and professional buildings. Most of the graduates set up law practices and the medical students did their internships and set up practices in the surrounding areas.

As did, Deanna's father and mother.

A very special friendship began to develop between everybody over the course of the next few years. That little coffee house became their hang out. Michael and Manerva would often talk about their roots, and Deanna seem to blend right in with hers. It made no difference that they each were different. Deanna, would always tease Manerva because it became obvious early on that Michael found her very attractive. Even though Manerva found Michael attractive also and really fell for him, she knew Deanna and her family cared for him also.

Deanna, would always say Michael was like the brother she loss. The brother her father had a chance to be like a father to again. Both Michael's parents had recently died also. He was on a mission to make them proud of him. Besides her roommate Alison, back in medical school in Memphis, Manerva had met a lot of people but Deanna like Alison had proved to be a special friend almost like a sister. They were the type of friends Manerva knew didn't come along everyday and were worth cherishing. Neither Deanna or Alison were black and neither treated her or any one she knew any different. In fact, both had treated her better than some of her oldest and childhood friends. Both had shared their hearts and their families with her and that to Manerva was a bond for life. A bond that she would forever remember and always honor.

A bond she and Michael would always remember and honor...

She and Michael had both agreed on that, after they were over the Sumner's home for dinner five years ago and overheard Dr. and Mrs. Sumner's conversation in the kitchen. Neither Dr. nor Mrs. Sumner had realized that Manerva and Michael were standing on the other side of the door while they were talking in the kitchen. Manerva and Michael had both gone to check on them because Mrs. Sumner had become sad and upset all of a sudden. Deanna, had gone upstairs to get something, she said she knew what would cheer her mom up. Unknowing to neither Michael nor Manerva was that the next day marked the anniversary of their son, his girlfriend and their unborn child all killed in a tragic car accident.

Dr. Sumner had placed his arms around Mrs. Sumner comforting her because she was crying so.

Manerva and Michael both were walking from the living room to see about them when they both overheard Mrs. Sumner almost shout out,

"Wayne, go back in there; I'll be back in shortly. They are such a beautiful couple, and I have grown to love both of them. I know they are both friends of Deanna, it's just that, tonight for the first time when Michael was hugging Deanna, I saw something different. I saw Michael and Deanna as a couple. I saw us having a second chance. A chance we didn't have with our son, because he never told us he had fallen in love and wanted to marry or about to become a father. We may have had a grandchild. We never shared all of the interracial issues we had. It may have been different because I wasn't black like her, I was Asian, nevertheless there was so much prejudice. So much hurt! Maybe if it were Michael and Deanna, I could let go some of the guilt I have wondering if we really ever let him know, that it didn't matter if she was different. I hurt so because I wonder if, we really let him know, all that really mattered was his happiness," Mrs. Sumner said.

"Honey, I know this is hard on you, it's been hard on me too, but that's not fair to them. I too would be a very happy man, if it were Michael and Deanna, but it is not. And frankly, we both love Manerva too and she and Michel really belong together. There are so many things, I would wish for, but we need to be happy for what we do have. We have a beautiful daughter, that is hurting too, but she has good friends that love her and we love them," Dr. Sumner said as he hugged and comforted his wife.

"Michael and I had heard enough, we both turned around and saw Deanna coming down the stairs with a photo album. A few minutes later, Dr. and Mrs. Sumner came out of the kitchen with a sticky rice dish Mrs. Sumner had made. It was one of her favorites. Michael loved it, so she had made an extra dish that he could take with him.

After dinner, and later that night Michael called me on the telephone. Somehow, we both knew what needed to be said. We both agreed."

"Manerva, I love you and I know you love me too, even though we have always kept it on a friendship level. I think my love and respect for you has grown more because of that! If we are meant to be, it will be the test of time. What I am about to say, really is not because I need the approval of anyone other than what I feel in my heart. But I have to be honest, I thank God I still have the memories of both my parents in my heart. I thank God for the good people that he have placed in my life that has helped me so.

I am not saying this just because of over hearing Dr. and Mrs. Sumner talking tonight, but I am going to say what I'm going to say because of the hurt that their son must have had not being able for what ever reason to go to them and tell them his wants and his desires and his dreams. It could have made a difference in their lives. It made me realize that I did share my hopes, my dreams and my desires with both my parents before they died and that is what drives me now. So, I must continue trying to reach those hopes, dreams and desires for them to make a difference. You have shared with me your hopes, your dreams, and your desires. So, you must also. We, must each, do what we have to do, to make a difference. Being together, right now, would hold us back. Whether we say it or not, we both know it. And, if the time comes *Manerva Ruthie Jones* that we still want each other and healing has been replaced by our accomplishments for so many, and if it is meant, we will be together. I just hope you understand. *Manerva* live your life as you must. Don't wait on me. Just know, as I know, if it is meant we will be together. I'll always love you!" Michael warmly explained to Manerva.

"I'll always, love you too *Michael.* Yes, I do understand. I've always understood. Even before I met you I understood. I think before I was even born, I understood. I've got one whole heart that will always love you. Always remember that *Michael Charles Glenn.* Go and do what you must do! Your mom and dad are proud of you and so am I," Manerva said softly as tears of sweetness fell with every word that she said before she hung up the telephone. *Then without saying or doing anything else she thanked God for Michael, rolled over and went sound asleep.*

There was an unspoken understanding that Manerva sensed in Deanna. In a lot of ways she saw a lot of herself in Deanna. Deanna's family had sort of become Manerva's transposed family away from home. They filled a void in Manerva's life. Sometimes on occasion Manerva would be alone and thinking. Especially doing the first couple of years she had left Memphis and was in the big city of Chicago. And often when she thought about Michael and how she had missed him not being in her life.

Manerva was a people person and was always meeting new people. She talked to different people on her jobs, in school and also continued to date. She still enjoyed having her private moments and her private thoughts. This was a thought she sometimes smiled about, because when she undressed there it was, big, brown, bold and beautiful, *her other heart.*

There it is starring right at me...

I do have two hearts, just like mama always would say. She always told me that God gave me one I could always see and one

I couldn't. She said I always had an extra heart to give and receive love! Mama, use to tell me about it, before I knew I even had it. I remember it grew as I grew. I have always wondered if there really is any truth to all of what she says. I just remember mama calling me Dollbaby and rocking me as a baby and even telling me it was my birthmark, and I should never forget it! And I never have! God gave it to me because I was so special. And I would always have it when I needed it most! I used to smile when I saw it growing up and often wondered did others have birthmarks as well? Come to think of it I'm sure God made others just as special as me.

Chapter Six

Homemade Biscuits and Black Berry Cobbler! Sands, Mississippi, 1951

Andrew T. Jones was a young pastor, who enjoyed visiting churches and preaching his sermons. He liked moving around. He had been preaching for about five years. He didn't have his own church and people would still say.

"That young man is going to be somebody, someday!" Folks from all over would say that. Whether they knew him or not. Once you got around him, you just knew it.

All Andrew knew was he loved talking about and spreading the word about God all over. He loved his mother, Mrs. Ruthie Jones too. "Mama, don't worry, I'll make you the best son ever, and make you proud of me," he would say to her many times.

"I'm already proud of everything you do, son," Mrs. Ruthie would always say back. Andrew had a nickname because his skin was such a light complexion and he radiated so. It was Sonnie, and he had a zest for life. He would get up early every morning before dawn and help with the chores around the farm. He knew the only person that got up before him each morning was Mrs. Ruthie.

Andrew loved to wake up to the smell of her homemade biscuits, freshly cured pork jowl, and black strap molasses *those were the thick, dark kind he would use to sop up with on his plate*. "I'm going to the barn, mama, and I'll chop you some wood on my way back," he said often.

"Just sit it in a pile next to the stove and fireplace, son," Mrs. Ruthie proudly said back while standing on the other side of the stove lifting the black iron sockets and placing wood down inside. "Got to make sure I keep my fire hot enough," she said also. Sometimes Mrs. Ruthie would just stand smiling and working as she looked out of the small back window over the stove. She could see her Sonnie going out back first to the pig pen and feed them the slop out of the bucket. He would then walk pass the well out back and lift up the wire fence into the pasture that led to the barn.

"Mama, I sat the basket of eggs on the porch. I'm going to check on "old Ben," said Sonnie as he walked along side the kitchen outside.

"Come in and eat your breakfast, before you start the crops, do you hear me Sonnie?"

"Yes, ma'am mama, I smell all that good food and I'm hurrying as fast as I can," said Sonnie. Sometimes, depending on how hungry she thought her boys were Mrs. Ruthie would have everything cooked. They loved her cooking especially her sweets, so she would have peach, apple, strawberry, blackberry cobblers, lemon and chocolate pies, you name it-she made it. Before he ate breakfast Sonnie would either drive the tractor or take his favorite mule *old Ben* and *his buggy* to see about the crops and live stock first. They owned quite a lot of land in Sands, Mississippi. They grew everything from watermelons, beans, peas, corn, cotton, and much more.

Andrew was the man of the house...

His father Lonnie B. Jones had died when he was in the ninth grade. Andrew's younger brother Junior was eight years younger than him. Junior was so young when their father died that Andrew was really the only father figure he knew. Andrew made sure he set a good example for him and made sure he taught him everything he needed to know about running a farm. Back then, it wasn't easy trying to go to school and being successful on the farm too. Most of Andrew's friends in school and church had to drop out and help on the farm. So Andrew was very appreciative of the many sacrifices Mrs. Ruthie had made to make sure he stayed in school, graduated and got his diploma. That's why until Junior graduated Andrew vowed he would take care of everything like his dad had.

Junior loved his big brother and wanted to help him so much. He was a fast learner and was determined to help Andrew with the chores before he went to school. But Andrew didn't want Junior to be too tired and worn out before he got to school, because he knew he had to walk to there neighbor's house and go with them. They lived a half mile down the road. The neighbors had an old truck and a buggy that they rotated driving into town. The school was just outside of town, and town was six miles. They had good neighbors and they would stop by often when they were going to town; to see if Mrs. Ruthie and her sons needed anything. Everybody loved Mrs. Ruthie and she could do almost anything except drive. Lonnie B. had taken good care of her and took her anywhere she wanted to go. He even took her to church every Sunday and went back and picked her up.

She was the town's seamstress and she was good. She would make her own patterns if she needed one by cutting out pages from the Sears Roebuck Catalog; in fact this wish book was used for almost everything including lining the outside outhouse walls. Mrs. Ruthie told Sonnie and Junior, "It just makes good sense, that while you sitting and waiting you could be looking and wishing." In addition to doing her own family's work sewing, canning jars of preserves and jellies and more, to make some extra money she would work and do it for others all over town. People would come from all over to drop off and pick up. If they didn't have the money they would trade almost any and everything. They never wanted Mrs. Ruthie to work for free.

Thanks to Mrs. Ruthie, especially after Lonnie B. died, she didn't have to pay for nearly anything. No doctor or dentist bills, no lawyer bills, nearly nothing. Lonnie B. had been a good provider and believed in paying cash or getting things on time. She was a very talented women and had a strong inner spirit, both her sons wanted to be there and protect her. She was an usher at their church and later got on the mother's board. Some Sunday's she would even teach Sunday School. Most Sundays, the pastor and many church members just happen to always be passing through and would stop by.

Mrs. Ruthie always had a lot of food cooked even before Lonnie B. died. One of her favorite meals was her fresh picked purple hulled peas, hot water cornbread, fried okra and tomatoes, fried corn, fried chicken, blackberry cobbler, lemon pie, chocolate cake and homemade ice cream. In case you ate too much, she always had an extra bed already fluffed with hand-made cotton or feathered mattress, hand made embroidered sheets and quilts. People use to say they felt like they were in heaven when they came over. Mrs. Ruthie was so proud of both her sons. Everyone would constantly tell her, "Ruthie, you are one blessed women!"

She would just smile back and say, "I just thank God!" After Junior graduated and got his diploma, he basically took over Andrews chores and became one of the best farmers in the area.

Things just happened the way she figured God wanted them to, and neither she nor Junior were surprised when the three of them were eating dinner and Andrew said, "Mama, Junior, I think God has a calling on me to preach!" "It's just something inside of me, that want let me stop telling people how good God is and how they need to accept and believe in him," Andrew said. When Andrew didn't hear a word, but saw tears rolling down first Mrs. Ruthie's cheeks then Junior, he knew. He knew they were happy for him but just didn't want to see him go. He has that spirit and fire in him that they knew wouldn't let him stop until he had made something of himself and done what God wanted him to do.

"All I can say is, you have been a good son and your daddy would be proud of you. I know he would tell me, Ruthie, just let him go, God will be with him, a man's got to do what a man's got to do. Just be happy son and know we love you," Mrs. Ruthie said.

"Bro, don't worry, I'll take care of mama and everything, you go on and preach," said Junior.

Mrs. Ruthie had made up in her mind then, she wouldn't try to stop him but give him her blessing. Andrew got up and hugged and prayed with both of them. He was so happy.

One Sunday, a couple of months later...

Andrew told Mrs. Ruthie, "Mama, I'm going to visit and preach at a church in Milton, Alabama." "It's about an hour drive from Sands," he said. He had worked hard and got a good deal on an old Ford pick up truck. It wasn't the best looking truck, but it had a good motor. Andrew was very smart and picked up on things very quick. Where ever he would go, he would watch and pick up on as much as he could. Lonnie B. had taught him to be quick with the eye, and trust your gut feelings to figure out things.

Once that old pick up truck had stopped and Andrew raised the hood and figured out how to fix it from watching other men working on cars and trucks in town. So, he felt confident he wouldn't have any problems with his old Ford pick up truck. When Andrew felt confident, Mrs. Ruthie and Junior didn't worry.

Andrew had a gut feeling it would be a special Sunday, but he didn't know exactly why? This church was a little larger than the one he belonged to, and they had about twenty more people in the congregation. The church was down a hill and there was no where to park his truck except at the end of the road and walk down. This was fine with Andrew because everybody mostly walked to church anyway. He got to church early and he had a good feeling walking down the road and seeing so many women caring dishes, speaking and smiling.

They didn't know who he was and he didn't say, as he nodded his head back smiling.

"Morning," they would say as they passed him, with a most curious look on their faces.

"A beautiful morning in deed ladies," he said back.

As he entered the church, he was greeted by an usher, wearing white gloves and motioning to an empty pew, he politely smiled and asked, "Where was the Pastor's study; he needed to read over some scriptures before service." About the same time the usher was walking him down the aisle; the Pastor opened the study door and saw him.

He immediately walked down the aisle smiling, "Morning Pastor Jones, glad you could make it. Come on back, make yourself at home, here is the study. We are just finishing up with a brief deacon's meeting. I haven't told anybody about you, I wanted it to be a surprise. They probably think you are a visiting deacon. Today is the Church's twentieth year anniversary, and for twenty years, I have always preached the sermon, well, you are my surprise to the church today, it's time for some young blood, and I want to sit back and enjoy you preach today. I told my wife about you the other Sunday. We haven't had a young preacher like you around here since I started preaching here twenty years ago. We are just so proud to have you here," said the Pastor of the Church. "You go on back and get ready; we will open for devotion in about fifteen minutes.

Andrew's sermon went very well. He felt good and the Holy Spirit was with him. Two new candidates for baptism had joined the church during his sermon. One was a young twelve year old boy and the other was a ninety five year old man. The baptizing was to take place the next Sunday in a creek located behind the church.

"We would love for you to come back, next Sunday to perform the baptism," the Pastor of the church said to Andrew. "I have known Brother Tommy for almost fifty years, and I thank God he used you to touch him to want to be baptized. He would always tell me, not to worry about him; God wasn't going to let him into heaven until he got baptized. And he wasn't getting baptized until he got good and ready. And for me to stop bothering him," said the Pastor again. "Let's go back in the kitchen, the women of the church have prepared a big dinner and they are ready to serve." The Pastor of the Church said.

Andrew said, "I'm ready to eat."...

Almost all the women in the church brought a dish. It smelled so good inside that Church and Andrew had worked up a big appetite. As they walked, in the back room of the church, there was a wood burning stove, an ice box, and three long bench tables on both sides of the church. Within minutes while they were sitting there, that small room changed into looking like a different place. Food came from everywhere and everything was arranged so neatly on beautiful white tablecloths and fine hand painted plates and saucers. The women of the church had done a good job preparing and setting everything up.

Andrew noticed that one of the usher's had given him special attention since the moment he had arrived. She was the same usher that had greeted him at the door and showed him the Pastor's Study. She had made sure he had plenty of water during the service. She had even told him not to leave after the service because they were going to have food prepared. Andrew knew she was a good usher and doing her job, but he also knew there was something special about her also. Now, she wanted to find out what he wanted on his plate? It was obvious, she wanted Andrew to be happy, and she didn't mind serving him. Andrew thought she was one of the nicest ushers he had seen, and the prettiest also.

He asked her, "What dish did you bring?"

She softly answered, "The Blackberry Cobbler."

Andrew then told her, "Give me a little of everything, and a lot of blackberry cobbler." She smiled.

Chapter Seven

Mama and Daddy!

When she returned with his plate, he thanked her and asked, "Sister, may I ask what is your name?"

She said, "Emma Mae Fields."

"Sister Emma Mae Fields, I would like to thank you for being so kind, and might I add, the food was delicious, especially the blackberry cobbler," he said. "Do you visit other churches?"

"If you will be preaching, I Will," said Emma smiling timidly.

Andrew continued to look and smiled. You could say it was almost love at first sight.

So it came to pass...

That after a year of courtship Pastor Andrew and Sister Emma became husband and wife. They lived with Mrs. Ruthie until they felt it was time to leave. Emma wanted so much to be able to be the kind of wife Andrew needed and wanted. She realized he had been raised by a very talented woman who she admired very much. She learned a lot from Mrs. Ruthie and tried to follow in her footsteps as much as she could knowing it wouldn't be easy.

Emma's mama had died while giving birth and her father had run off when she was a baby. Emma was raised by her grandparents. They had both gotten very old but they loved Emma has if she was their very own. Emma loved them so and always made sure she checked on them. Emma was determined to try and do everything within her power to make Andrew and Mrs. Ruthie happy and proud of her also. Andrew loved Emma, and he thought she was so beautiful.

He often told her, "Emma, God sure made a beautiful woman when he made you. You were the prettiest lady at church that day. I couldn't stop looking at your beautiful skin and eyes. I had to ask God to forgive me that day because you looked better than your blackberry cobbler to me even under your white usher's dress."

"You, better stop talking like that Andrew Jones; you know what that kind of talk do to me," Emma would always say.

"Well, just walk those big, pretty legs over here and show me, Mrs. Emma Mae Jones," he would say back. And when she did, he wouldn't say much more than, "Come here woman!" He would then start kissing her full red lips, and before she knew it even though he wasn't a very big man himself, he would just pick up her five foot two, one hundred and twenty pound body and lay her across the bed. She totally captivated him.

It was doing these times that Andrew and Emma appreciated that Andrew and Junior had built them an entire new room on the outside of the house on the side of the back porch. When their door was closed you couldn't hear a thing from within or outside of their room.

Mrs. Ruthie showed Emma everything she knew how to do including sewing, canning and basically how to oversee a household. Emma was a quick learner and had a lot of talent of her own. Emma learned all of Andrew's favorite dishes. In many ways Emma started to love Mrs. Ruthie and was like the daughter she never had. Andrew realized this and he was pleased.

Andrew and Junior both worked hard doing whatever odd jobs they could to help modernize Mrs. Ruthie's house. She was so happy when she no longer had to pump water from their well or go out back to the outside outhouse. This was a very big accomplishment not only for black people but for all people living in that area. Mrs. Ruthie appreciated her family so. People still talked all around of how blessed Mrs. Ruthie was. She was even the first in the area to get a telephone and a black and white TV. Mrs. Ruthie would joke for days because she never could get use to having a party line and hearing other people's conversation when she picked up the telephone.

She and Emma still believed in not saying any of their business over the telephone but it came in handy if there was an emergency in the area. People would even just stop by and leave Mrs. Ruthie and Emma money and food sitting by the telephone and TV. They were so appreciative that anytime anyone would stop by, they would go back and make sure the messages got to the right people. Their home was almost like a townhouse away from town.

December nineteen hundred and fifty two...

Andrew and Emma decided to move and go to the big city of Memphis, TN and settle down. He felt he could eventually help start his own church; they could buy their own house, and start having their own big family. He always had a secret desire of having a sister or a girl around the house growing up, so this was his chance to have his own daughter if it was God's will. He and Emma had already decided if they ever had a little girl what the name would be.

"They say my mother's name was Manerva and deep down, I have always liked the name Manerva, I use to wish I was named after my mother, to me it sounds so special," said Emma."

"Emma sounds special enough for me," said Andrew. "And you're special to me," Andrew said.

"Then, how would Manerva Ruthie Jones for our little one sound to you?" asked Emma.

"I love it! And so it will be! Thank you Emma, for wanting and claiming God to grant my desire even before it happens," said Andrew smiling with great pleasure.

"Andrew, God knows our hearts and our desires, and to me if he so wills, she will be a blessing from God and my little doll baby," Emma said as they both hug and kiss one another, ceasing from discussing anything else.

January, nineteen hundred and fifty three. Mr. and Mrs. Andrew T. Jones with their old Ford pick up truck, a full tank of gas, two suitcases filled with clothes, plenty of food, Andrew's black bible, everybody's blessings, a whole lot of love and twenty dollars, set off to go to Memphis, Tennessee.

A short while later

Manerva hears her office telephone rang. "Good the caller ID is showing that Deanna is calling me back. Enough of me thinking about me being special and my birthmark. I'm still at work on this cold snowy Chicago Friday evening!" Manerva thought as she answered the telephone. "Hello Deanna, did you forget to tell me something," Manerva said jokingly.

"Manerva, are things alright with Katherine-Jean? Deanne asked showing concern in her voice.

"Deanna, you know you keep up with everything more than I do, and remember Katherine-Jean has been out of town this past week with her family. Did you forget or are you just as nervous as I am about Saturday night or are you starting to become a little senile?" Manerva said. "I'm glad you called me back, because I was about to call you anyway. I won't make it to the gym tonight. I want to go over some things I just found out regarding the big case I'm meeting about in about an hour. Plus, I need to sort out a lot of things, going on. You know I work better when I can think with a clear mind. I don't think Kenneth will be back in town tonight. Michael has left me a voice mail that he can't wait to see me Saturday night. That has really thrown me off guard," said Manerva.

"Hold on a minute Manerva! That's why I called you back. To give you heads up! Katherine-Jean is on her way to see you now! You wouldn't let me get a word in on this call," said Deanna.

"What?" asked Manerva? "I don't have an appointment or any meeting scheduled with Katherine-Jean on today that I know about. I've got a briefing here with my neighbor Dr. Parks in fifteen minutes and an advisory board meeting at the hospital at four o'clock today that I absolutely can't miss. Are you sure?" Manerva asked again.

"The only reason I know, is because I just passed her home, and saw her getting into her car. Well, you know me and I thought she was out of town also. Plus, you know Katherine-Jean usually doesn't drive and especially not in this weather even if the streets are cleared, so I called her from my car phone. She sounded upset and not herself, I could tell she had been crying. She told me she would talk to me later; and that she was on her way to see you first to discuss some things. I knew you never mentioned anything about it, and we had talked several times earlier," said Deanna.

"Deanna, I need you to do me a favor. I am meeting my neighbor here downstairs now to do a briefing before the big meeting in about an hour at the hospital. Your dad is still at the office, would you call him and call Donna our receptionist and tell her if Katherine-Jean comes in to see me, ask her to just wait in my office, I should be back within an hour and a half. If it is an urgent matter and it can't be prolonged, tell her to go and talk to your dad," said Manerva.

"Manerva go take care of your meetings, I'll handle talking to my dad and Donna, and I just wanted you to know beforehand! Go! Go!" Deanna said.

Moments later...

"Hi dad, need you to do a favor!" said Deanna. "Don't have the details, but if Katherine-Jean comes to the office before Manerva gets back from her advisory board meeting at the hospital in about an hour and a half, would you talk to her. All, I know is she's on her way and she's very upset. I think she may need legal counseling, that's just my gut feeling," Deanna said.

"Honey sounds like I just heard someone come in and talking at the desk, I'm finished for the day, I'll go out and talk to her," Dr. Sumner said while walking to his door and hanging up the phone with his daughter. "Hello Katherine-Jean, what a pleasant surprise," Dr. Sumner said as he walked out of his office and over toward Katherine-Jean. Donna, thanks, I'll take this. I could hear Katherine-Jean when she came in from my office. Ms. Jones will be returning from her meeting in about an hour or so, why don't you step into my office while you wait and tell me how you and your lovely family been doing," said Dr. Sumner. It's cold outside, I don't make the best but let me fix you a hot cup of chocolate, he said while smiling at Katherine-Jean.

"Thank You Dr. Sumner. That sounds nice," Katherine-Jean said as she seemed to relax and give a warm smile back.

Walking her into his office he immediately pulled over a chair from his desk for Katherine-Jean to sit down in. His daughter's assessment of how upset Katherine-Jean appeared to be was absolutely correct. He was determined to try and get her to relax as soon and as much as possible. "Like I said I don't make the best hot chocolate in town, but I manage," He said. "I've been here since about 4:00am this morning and have had a long day and drank too many cups of coffee so I need to switch up anyway and have myself a cup of hot chocolate as well," Dr. Sumner said.

"A cup of hot chocolate would do wonders right now, but let me make it for you, I insist," Katherine-Jean said calmly. I feel like I need to keep moving and doing things" she said.

"Please forgive me for prying but has something happened, you need to talk about?" Dr. Sumner asked as he sat down and pulled another chair beside her. "I only ask because it's not everyday someone comes through the rush hour traffic close to three in the afternoon, in six or more inches of snow without wearing at least a sweater, not even a friend, unless there is something heavy on their mind," he said with a gentle smile. "I know I'm not Manerva, but you are a friend of the family. I do have a listening ear my dear and it will be kept confidential even to my daughter Deanna or my wife unless you tell me otherwise," he said.

"Thank You Dr. Sumner, it's just so much and I don't know where to start. Manerva doesn't even know nor have a clue of what I want to tell her," she said.

"First, you just need to relax and unwind," Dr. Sumner told her with genuine concern. "Just make yourself comfortable. Remember, you use to work here. It may have been several years ago, but I'll never forget how you helped my wife out and helped me stay organized. You are still like family to us. In fact, the other office is empty if you would like to just go in there and be alone for awhile or even take a nap. The sofas still let out to really comfortable beds in each of the offices. Our other law partner is out of town for the next couple of weeks," Dr. Sumner said. "When you are ready, you just start from the beginning," he said giving her a box of kleenex. "Here is your hot chocolate, let me get my cup of coffee and I'll be right with you," he said smiling.

"Dr. Sumner, I've given everyone the impression that I have this perfect marriage. I've worked so hard to try to make it work and I don't know what to do? Everything is based on lies," she said.

"Let me stop you and tell you a little story Katherine-Jean, one that only a few people know. People probably wouldn't understand and would make fun of me and my family if they knew but I'm proud of it. I don't want you to think I'll judge you because who am I to judge anyone. When people look at me now all they see is by their measures of success that I'm both a doctor and a lawyer. I've had to sacrifice a lot and made a lot of decisions and the one thing I know is that I don't have any regrets because of it, I've had to fight to keep my family together and that's all that matters," Dr. Sumner said.

"Back when my wife and I first were first married we had no money and we had to use all public services that were available and free. I'm not knocking public services at all, I'm just saying being a foreigner and being broke I had no choice. We had just come to the United States to live. All I knew I had was a wife pregnant with twins at the time. I know we were told that because of sloppy delivery practices both our babies died and my wife almost died. They never let us see our twins nor knew what happened. When we tried to inquire, we were simple told nothing.

My wife had become sick and didn't want to go to the hospital to begin with. She knew an old lady from her homeland who was a mid-wife but we didn't have the money to send for her. I am Italian and my wife is of Asian descent. We often wondered did that have anything to do with it. We still experience a prejudice because of our cultures. I could tell you stories that would tear your heart apart. We experienced it all over before and after we arrived here in the United States. Some of our own cultures disowned us because back then they claimed we disgraced our families by mixing blood and because we left our homelands. Both of our families were well off but we returned married we were denounced and rejected.

When we came...

To the United States we encountered besides the prejudice of cultures and nationalities we experienced how it felt to be broke. We were not allowed to do all work or go to some schools even though we passed all the test and requirements. I made a vow to my wife after we lost both our babies and she almost died that I would do whatever work I could and send myself to school by whatever means, so the next time I could help deliver our children. I did jobs and things that I am not very proud of and had to ask God for forgiveness. I felt I had no choice if my family was to survive," Dr. Sumner shared with sadness in his eyes.

"So I did, and eventually formed a group of medical professions that would actually go out to a woman's home and follow her delivery from start to finish in their own homes. Years later, I helped deliver my daughter Deanna and my son Toney. I then ran into so many legal and political loop holes that didn't make sense to me, that when I went back to school and passed the board exams and became a lawyer. I mention this story to you because I know firsthand how important family is and what a person will or will not do to keep their family together.

With all that said, my son had some problems and I was so busy I didn't see it. Afterwards I realized he had come to my office many times and for what ever reason, I wish I had given him a cup of hot chocolate or listened. It may have saved his life. It may have saved their lives. He, his girlfriend and their unborn child was killed in a tragic car accident. He would have been about your age. We never knew about his girlfriend. When we went to the scene, all we could tell was how beautiful they all were in the midst of all. Whatever happened it seemed as though somehow they were together. The police had called us to the scene and somehow even though they had to cut to get to them both of their bodies were together and both of their personal belongings were all inside a new baby's diaper bag. It looked like they had gone shopping because there were bags of other new baby items with tags still on them. The diaper bag was new with a tag on it but her purse and my son's jacket and cell phone was zipped up inside. The diaper bag was sitting between both of them. Her skin tone was about the same as yours. She was petite with think black hair that she wore in a pony tail. Looking at her that day she looked like my mom when she was young dressed in her ballerina outfit and her long brunette ponytail. Maybe Toney saw that too? Maybe that was one of the things that attracted him to her? We could have grandchildren, but we'll never know? So, please don't think I will judge you for anything Katherine-Jean?" Dr. Sumner finished saying as he looked up and saw tears from Katherine-Jeans eyes.

"Dr. Sumner, you are God sent, your story, is so touching, and you hit on some things that I have often wondered about me or my husband? We have each made some decisions that may have not been right but they were made with the hope of keeping our family together. That's why it's so hard now. Knowing if the truth comes out, it could destroy my children and knowing that in the sight of God how can we keep living lies. I think I have turned to Manerva, more through the years that I have known her for her guidance in always wanting to do the right things. I'm not saying she is perfect, but she has a good heart. I think also because of her strength and determination. Being a strong ambitious black woman also, I know she understand a lot of the struggles I have had to go through.

Dr. Sumner, I think I admire Manerva most because she has shown me that you should never settle or compromise your beliefs, no matter what. In a lot of ways, I am very ashamed because Mrs. Sumner and you have been there and helped me through some very bad times, not knowing the whole story. I wanted to tell you both, I just didn't know how. Things of my past, my children's past, that if told will effect their future. I have done things for good reasons, feeling like I had no other choices also. I feel my family will suffer because of those choices. Most importantly, forgiveness is needed. Dr. Sumner, I received papers today that my husband has filed for a divorce, and wants full custody of my children. Both of us have kept horrible things inside. Dr. Sumner would you and Manerva represent me to keep my children?" Katherine-Jean asked.

"Katherine-Jean, it is easier said than done, but I don't want you to worry. Yes, I would be honored to represent you. I can't speak for Manerva, but I feel confident she will feel the same way. Do you want to talk to her first, or do you want me to talk to her?" he said.

"Dr. Sumner, thank you, I feel much better now, Manerva has enough on her that's why I didn't call her or leave a message, I know it would only upset her; I just wanted to come and talk. It will be fine if you see her before I do, to tell her, she will understand. You have my permission to mention it to Deanna and Mrs. Sumner as well, Deanna saw me briefly and I wasn't myself, please let her know I'm alright. When I see her I'll talk to her as well. She and Mrs. Sumner have been like family to me. I know they nor Manerva would judge me, it's just hard for me to face reality that it's time to tell it all."

"Well, you don't have to do it all today, and you've got friends that love you and those beautiful children." he said, hugging her good bye.

"Oh, before I leave, just one more thing Dr. Sumner, Congratulations to you, before your big night on Saturday, don't worry, I'll be there with bells on," Katherine-Jean said.

"Glad you could make it a few minutes early, Ms. Jones, what is your overall opinion regarding the case?" asked one of her clients. "In all honesty, after looking at all of the evidence, it's still a little early in the game to say. Let's hear all sides to report in the meeting. Let's see what they are officially charging and what they are looking for? Can you tell me exactly what happened, in your own words," asked Manerva. "Yes, it all started..." said the client as they were walking into the board room.

Manerva was sitting at this meeting and hearing all of the different versions of what happened that night. She was actually consulting on the side that she knew would surely win the case. She should be very happy to be on a winning team. To have this type of publicity headlined on the front page of the *Chicago Tribune* and all the other papers would do wonders for her career. To be noted at all on this win plus mentioned at the banquet on Saturday night would give her career the political boost she had worked so hard for. Chicago was known for its politics. And being a black woman on the winning side could assure Manerva a winning ticket to do whatever she chose to do. So why did all this have such a mind boggling effect on the inside of her?

Until her friend and neighbor Dr. Parks, who just happened to also be the medical examiner working with this case came by earlier and showed her the autopsy report earlier, she was prepared to present a case to ask for a settlement to prevent any license or medical credentials to be revoked. The court date had been ordered to be set within thirty days. Her client's entire version of what had happened the night the patient died collaborated exactly with what was written in the findings of the autopsy report. There was really no case. She would not be surprised if the judge dismissed the case before the thirty days entirely. Now, she understood what Dr. Parks had said earlier, *Things are not adding up.*

Dr. Parks had been asked to take over the position as the consulting medical examiner, after the original person had suffered a stroke and died three months ago. She had shared so many stories with Manerva of what she had to go through to be heard and get pass *The little boys club.*

"I have always admired her so, because many times when she would say things of that nature, that's when her husband would seem to comfort her and say.

"Honey, those are the things, I don't miss, you know you can just leave; you don't have to take all that."

She would always say back, "*I know, dear, but this is not your fight.*"

He and I both knew, what she meant. She wanted to make a difference, the best and only way she could.

"I loved being around her, because I drew so much strength and found out just being a women had its own share of fights no matter what color you were or where you came from," Manerva thought and reflected on silently.

One of the things Dr. Parks had shown me...

Was that knowing where you came from prepared you for where you wanted to go. As Manerva, left the meeting, she reached inside her daytimer portfolio case and checked her 2-way radio, pager and cell phone. This plus her laptop was her office as she traveled. Almost everything she needed was within her reach. She liked that. She had turned everything on silent and forwarded all her calls to her secretary Donna. It was almost five thirty and she had received no new calls.

"No calls from Katherine-Jean, I wonder did she stop by my office or waiting to see me at the gym tonight. I'd better to check with the office because I'm not going to the gym tonight, I'm not even going walking, I'm exhausted. I'm going to go home and cuddle up and relax. I'm going to tune everybody out tonight except me, myself and I. I want to just soak in my hot jacuzzi bath and sit by the fireplace afterwards my hot cup of tea and read my new novel I just bought. That's what I want to do. Let me just call into my office first, I'm not even going to have the cab driver to stop there, I'm going straight home," she though to herself.

Even though the streets are cleared, and the traffic along the lakefront is moving at a snail's pace, it's probably worse down any of the side streets. It's amazing that in Chicago, people go more in weather like this! They never stop going or slow down.

"Hi, Donna, my meeting went a little longer than I had planned, I'm exhausted. Do I have any messages and why are you still there? Would you retrieve all the messages from my voice mail?" Manerva asked.

"I wanted to make sure I caught up on all my work here, Ms. Jones, don't worry. I'm waiting on my husband to come pick me up. You only had one call, he said he was Congressman Glenn and he'll get to town earlier than expected. He asked me to check your schedule to see if you were free for breakfast tomorrow? I told him I wasn't sure, I would have to check with you? He left this telephone number and asked if I would tell you he will be staying at The Blake Hotel. He said there were a lot of delays at O'Hara but he should be at the hotel by eight o'clock tonight," said Donna.

"This is a surprise," Manerva said.

"Ms. Jones, may I ask is this the same Congressman Glenn that ran for the Mayor of Chicago, about five years ago?" asked Donna.

"Yes Donna, the same year I started working here," said Manerva thinking back.

"He should have won that election if you ask me, I sure voted for him. So many people voted for him, blacks and whites, he was a good man and very good looking too. Oh, Ms. Jones, Katherine-Jean came by the office shortly after you left, I had the feeling she had come to see you, but Dr. Sumner, came right out and took her into his office. She seemed upset at first but when she left she seemed OK. She just said, she would see you tonight," Donna said.

"Thanks Donna, I'll see Katherine-Jean. I don't know if I ever told you or if you know but Katherine-Jean, use to work here part time. She is a nurse. Long story, Mrs. Sumner is a nurse also. She had retired from Nursing and was the office manager here. She taught a few classes at the School of Nursing if they needed her, but she was determined to help Dr. Sumner stay organized. He's a brilliant man in all respects, but you know firsthand how he is with all his paperwork. Mrs. Sumner always had a good sense of people. Katherine-Jean was one of the other Nursing Instructors. She was in great financial and marital problems because her husband's company was going bankrupt. Mrs. Sumner hired Katherine-Jean part time to help her especially answer the telephones. Mrs. Sumner is a perfectionist and she is very soft spoken and being of Asian decent doesn't speak very good english. Dr. Sumner and Deanna take pride in telling the story of how Mrs. Sumner and Katherine-Jean literally saved her husband's suffering company and marriage working here. That's how Deanna and I met Katherine-Jean. She is a very special person. I'm glad that Dr. Sumner was there for her. She admires him like a father.

Oh, Donna, give me the telephone number Congressman Glenn left, and you get out of there and go home. I'll see you tomorrow," said Manerva.

Chapter Eight

What Do I Do?

Ring! Ring! Ring!...

"Hi Kathy, are you alright? I'm sorry, I wasn't at the office when you stopped by, I just called and Donna told me, you spoke to Dr. Sumner?" said Manerva

"Manerva, I'm better especially after talking to Dr. Sumner and the kids are fine!" Katherine-Jean said.

"You didn't mention Donald? Is everything alright? Anything you want to talk about?" asked Manerva.

"I'm sorry I was so upset I didn't call you before just coming to your office. Dr. Sumner heard me come in and at the desk talking to Donna. He came and got me immediately. He was the next best thing to you; he calmed me down and made me realize I've got to do the right thing. I need to start by telling you and Deanna the whole truth and nothing but the truth before everyone else finds out. Donald has filed for a divorce and thinks he's going to get custody of my children and my money!" said Katherine-Jean. I will kill him first!"

"Kathy, no you will not! Don't even think that! Where are you now?" asked Manerva.

"I'm about ten minutes from your office. The traffic was bumper to bumper, so I got off of the drive and decided to stop in this restaurant at the corner of Michigan Ave and Lake Street to calm my nerves, it all hit me and I realized I was driving, you know how I hate driving.

I would leave my car in this garage and take a cab home except I've got to pick the kids up from a soccer game at eight o'clock," Katherine-Jean said.

"Just stay, where you are, I'm five minutes away from there, I'll have my cabdriver turn off at Lake Street, which is the next exit coming up. Don't worry about the kids, I'll get Deanna to pick them up from the game and take them over her house, remember, she lives two blocks away from you. What are God Mothers for anyway! We keep telling you, you just birthed our children for us anyway!" Manerva said.

"Thanks Manerva, what can I say."

"Nothing, just stay where you are, we are almost at the exit, I'll see you in five minutes. This, is the only restaurant on this corner, it must be it, just wait five minutes, if I don't come back out, just leave and keep the change. There is her car, this is it, thanks," she said to the cabdriver as she got out of the cab and walked toward the restaurant.

All of the sidewalks were clear and free of snow...

Manerva had no problem rolling her little black cart with her laptop and all into the restaurant. She was actually familiar with this restaurant. She remembered she had been here a couple of times before for meetings. When she walked inside it was crowded with people. This entire area was so diverse, it was know as the area for *Progressive People*. People were doing literally everything. Some were meeting. Some were eating. Some were sitting alone working with their laptops on the tables or studying. Some were dancing. Some were on a platform center stage rehearsing plays and singing. Some were playing cards. Some were sitting at the bar drinking. You name it they were probably in there doing it. It was considered one of the happening spots in the area. It was also walking distance from downtown. Rumors were that Oprah had a penthouse a couple of blocks over near the Hancock Building.

As Manerva walked in, she glanced quickly all around, over to her right, sitting on a stool at the bar, she could see the side of young lady who even slightly bent over looking into her bag could easily have been mistaken to be Lena Horne. *Manerva knew it was Katherine-Jean.*

As she came closer, Katherine-Jean turned and looked and with a stillness said, "Manerva, I love you, come sit down, it's time you know the real me."

Manerva just put her arms around her, and they both embraced in a long hug. She then sat on a stool, and said, "Do any of us really know who we are? I wonder and struggle so many times looking for that answer. The best answer I've ever come up with is, there's only one person who really knows us, and he loves us despite anything we do because he knew we were going to do it before we did. So Kathy, what ever you have done, just know I love you and God loves you, Manerva said as she sat on a stool.

"I'm tired of Donald, holding this over my head, Manerva. I need you and Dr. Sumner to help me. I did wrong! And I've tried to make up for it every day of my life! I just don't want to loose my children! He can take the money, I don't care about that but not my children," Katherine-Jean said crying and becoming upset again.

"Kathy, let's move from this bar and sit at that empty table right over there, and first of all you relax! Then just start from the beginning. You've got to tell me everything, even if you don't think it is important. We will find a way to win this," said Manerva.

"It all started back when I met Donald in Arkansas in nineteen seventy five, twenty years ago. Everybody here just assumed I had this nice childhood, because of the facade we had worked hard at portraying and keeping up. Happy Upper Class Family. Husband—Caucasian—Successful Business Developer and Entrepreneur, Wife—Black—Beautiful Retired Nurse—Parents of Two Beautiful Children—A Daughter almost sixteen—who want to someday be a Doctor. A Son—almost twelve—who want to someday be just like his Dad. That picture I just painted sounded good, the only problem is it's all a lie. Well, not all of it, the children's dreams are real, that's why this all hurts so.

Donald had nothing, when I met him. I don't know what I must have been thinking. I never knew who my parents were, all my life the parents I thought were mine were not. I loved them and thought they loved me. I grew up an only child, always wanting other brothers and sisters. Anyway, I didn't find out they weren't my real parents until one hot southern night in Arkansas. This was during my fifth year of marriage to Donald. I loved him so and I had tried to be the wife he wanted and the daughter my parents wanted so. So here is the long story Manerva. The truth about it all. And it goes like this...

Once Upon A Time....

To this day I never understood, how they thought telling me I wasn't their real daughter and in the same breathe telling me how they and Donald had arranged for me to become pregnant in the same sentence was going to make me happy. I never knew I had been injected until after I woke up. I was unaware I had been given hot chocolate with sedatives that knocked me completely out. I remember vaguely dreaming of several doctors standing around me. The next morning after I woke up, I remember seeing both my so called parents and Donald sitting beside my bed talking. I remember them asking me how I felt and did I remember anything. I told them I didn't except seeing the doctors. They told me I had been injected with some of Donald's sperms to see if I could become pregnant that way.

We had tried almost everything known unsuccessfully for the previous five years. I remember beginning to feel different after about the third week. I went to the doctor and was told I was pregnant. I became so happy. It didn't take away the hurt of finding out they were not my real parents but it eased the pain to know I would have a child of my own to love. It was not until my doctor showed me later that some of my test results were very different than they had ever been before. I should have looked into it further then but just knowing I was almost in my eight month and about to finally deliver was all that I could think of. It was not until I had a miscarriage two years later that I overheard Donald and my parents talking one night about how thankful they were that he had found some frozen embryo cells whose mother had just become pregnant and had died in surgery or I would never have gotten pregnant.

They were bragging that it was perfect because the mother was black and the father was white and also that the father was one of the doctors who had come that night. They were bragging because they felt they had paid a good price for the implanted frozen embryo cells they had placed in me. One of the doctors knew Donald and how desperate he was for his wife to become pregnant. When I confronted Donald with this, he admitted everything and told me if I ever told or tried to leave him he would divorce me and take my child away because I had signed papers with my parents both as witnesses that same night I remember nothing about. Per Donald the papers stated that he was the natural father that had supplied the sperm and the mother had died in surgery and had wished to remain unknown prior. Donald told me I had signed stating I was only the acting surrogate mother who had volunteered for this rather new In vitro fertilization procedure only. Donald stated he and my parents had all the papers witnessed and notarized that after the baby was born I would give up all rights as an acting surrogate mother and return the child to its natural father who was Donald.

Being a nurse...

I had read articles on this new procedure that really became known about 1978. Several cases had been very successful. I had never thought about it as an option and was unaware Donald or my parents not only had heard of it but had arranged for it to be done and on me. They just used me and my body. The only thing I knew was that even in all the wrong, somehow God had worked his power through me of keeping life. Life to frozen embryo cells that grew within my body and one of those cells had become fertilized and stayed alive within my body. This is all I knew. I guess deep down, this is all I ever wanted to know. I was implanted that night fifteen years ago with frozen embryo cells. I remember having only one feeling the moment life started growing within me, *and that was love.* Nothing else mattered at that point. I never confronted my so called parents since they had paid Donald, signed those papers without telling me or getting my consent and setting up a trust fund for him to have control of all their businesses and money until each of my children became eighteen. They even put in a stipulation to make a game out of it all. I guess they always knew I would care more for my children than their money, so they never gave me any power or say so in the entire situation.

They knew if I ever was in a position to make a choice I would choose my children over the money. So they had it all worked out so Donald would be the one who had control of the trust fund even after my children turned eighteen as long as he remained their father prior to their eighteenth birthday. The only stipulation is if he is proved by law to be unworthy for any reason prior to each child becoming eighteen, then each child will have control of their own trust upon turning eighteen. I guess they figured they gave me and my children eighteen years to fight and play games with him and if we couldn't win over him in eighteen years he deserved it all. I guess they felt they had paid for me maybe the same way and I turned out alright. They got what they paid for with me, so why shouldn't Donald get what he paid for also.

I remember growing up and they would always make me play these competitive games for almost everything. Years later, I thought about some of the rumors I use to hear growing up, that our black maid was my father's mistress. I remember seeing younger pictures of her and thinking she was even more beautiful than Lena Horne. I remember my mother always telling me when I was a child how her own mother had been raped by one of their workers. I guess I always wanted to believe that explained how I could be their daughter and look a lot like Lena Horne as many would say or how two whites could have a mixed black daughter. Nothing else made sense. Nothing was really ever given to me even when I did deserve it.

Over the years of marriage Donald cheated and let me know he would take my daughter, the money and tell her I was not her mother unless I behaved as a wife to him and give him a son. So I just existed giving all my love to my daughter, and I became unfaithful once during my marriage. *During that time I really did become pregnant.* Donald found out I had been unfaithful and blood test were done. It turned out Donald was the real father. This gave him more ammunition against me. There were so many times I had dreamed about just leaving Donald, taking both my children and letting him have all the money. I never did for fear he would find me and out of revenge take them away legally and then take all their money.

About six years ago...

Was about the time his company had almost become bankrupt and I met Mrs. Sumner. He had threatened to take both of my children away, divorce me if I didn't help him get his business back up and running. From then until now all of the rest has been just history. Thank God I became friends with you and Deanna and I have been able to play the part better. I guess I felt I had other things to focus on and things were appearing alright at least for my children anyway. Donald has never loved them but he has been able to present himself as this very busy father totally devoted to his work.

Manerva, yesterday Donald had me served with divorce papers. He only wants a divorce now because Valerie will turn eighteen in less than two years and to eliminate any chance of me ever thinking that I might have any way of ever proving him unworthy he want to get full custody now. With Donald it has always been about the money. He cares nothing for the children. I use to think it was really because Valerie was really not his, but Brian is, and Manerva he cares nothing for Brian either. I don't care about the money, I never have. I want Valerie to know the truth and maybe find and know about her real parents. I owe her that! I'd like to give her what I never had!

I couldn't even think about this before because she feeling such a need for me in allowing me to be her mother. I have asked God for forgiveness so many times, because I have been selfish in loving her for sixteen years and I couldn't find the strength. It has only been since; I met you, that I've found the strength to let go and let God. You have always told me that, unknowing any of this.

Manerva! Manerva! Somebody help!...

"Somebody call 911! Help, please help!!!

Katherine-Jean was almost hysterical but managed to somehow keep it together somewhat and said, "She fell out, help me, lay her flat." By then everyone was there standing and bending trying to help.

"Would someone give me my bag over there, I'm a nurse." *OK, Katherine-Jean, you're a nurse, keep it together for Manerva, her conscious kept telling her.*

"Her vitals are fine, give me that small pack in that pouch please, it's smelling salt, I always carry some in case." *Oh my God, wake up Manerva, wake up!* While Katherine-Jean kept calling her name and telling her to wake up, Manerva started coughing struggled trying to talk and open her eyes.

"Don't try to talk, just relax, take some deep breaths, just relax," Katherine-Jean said to Manerva.

"I had this terrible dream, about you and the kids and then everything started getting blurry, my head started hurting really bad, I can't move my arm. I can't move my leg, *Roberta,* what's happening, talk to me *Roberta!* " Manerva said as she tried to raise her head to Katherine-Jean.

Katherine-Jean looking down trying to hold back the tears and shouting, "We need an ambulance! Somebody help us!"

"A voice of an older man from behind the bar shouted back, "They're on their way I just called!"

Katherine-Jean looked down and saw Manerva just lying back, *with eyes closed.*

With hands shaking...

She picked up Manerva's limp left arm and laid it down quickly.

Mumbling to herself, *"Who is Roberta? OK Kathie, you know what to do, do it! Manerva needs you. She can't be dead. Oh, God, help her, please help her,"* she said while wiping tears from her face.

She slowly bent over and tilted Manerva's head back and lifted her chin. This would allow her lungs to get air through her nose and mouth. She then looked for her chest to rise. She didn't see it move. She put her ear to her mouth and listened closely.

Then Katherine-Jean gently pressed her two fingers placed fingers on her neck to feel her pulse looking at her watch. *"Thank You Lord, I hear a pulse, its weak, but... "* she said just before she saw people moving and she heard.

"Coming through, stand back," said one of the paramedics.

Katherine-Jean quickly spoke up, "I'm a nurse, and her friend, everything happened all of a sudden, she just passed out and fell. I checked, she has a very weak pulse, no movement at all, spoke in confusion before she became unconscious."

As both the paramedics took over...

One placed his hand to support Manerva's head; he noticed blood on the floor and on the back of her head. As they performed all of the necessary test needed, one paramedic was on the radio to the hospital calling everything in.

Katherine-Jean had given them all the necessary information they needed and told them to take her to NorthCentral which was the closest and have them page Dr. Sumner and Dr. Parks. She couldn't really think who was On-Call but she knew Dr. Sumner and Dr. Parks would get the right people there.

As she was getting into the ambulance to ride with Manerva, she telephoned Deanna.

"Hello!"

"Hello Deanna, everything is happening so quickly, I'll tell you everything later. Look I don't want you worried, she will be fine, remember I'm a nurse; I'm on my way to NorthCentral in the ambulance with her now to have some test run," Katherine-Jean said.

"Wait a minute Katherine-Jean, you are not making any sense, who will be fine?" asked Deanna.

"Manerva! Deanna she just fainted over dinner. I'm sorry, let me calm down, everything happened so fast and you know its procedure to have x-rays and all done. I managed to keep her stable and take her vitals before the ambulance arrived."

"Oh, my God, look me and..."

"No, Deanna! You and my children just stay where you are! The paramedics gave her a sedative, to keep her calm. I'll be with her, I'll call you later and keep you posted. I should not have been hysterical when I called you. So much has happened today. Don't you worry about us? I need the pediatric godmother to take care of her godchildren tonight. I don't want them worried about me so just tell them Aunt Manerva has a problem and I'm spending the night with her. Tell them to just take their suitcases still already packed from our trip and spend the night with you. Oh Deanna, one more thing, I don't want Donald anywhere near my children. I'll explain later," she said as low as possible while sitting looking at Manerva.

"OK Nurse! You make sure everything is alright with Manerva, and don't you worry about this end, I'll take care of our children, tell Manerva we love her when she wakes up. She has been pushing herself too hard, being there for everybody else. Tell her to just relax. Got to go, here's a call coming in from your daughter now. I had told them to call me when they were ready to be picked up," Deanna said.

Deanna grabbed her keys and locked her door. *"Something awful was happening between Katherine-Jean and Donald, I sense it in Katherine-Jean's voice, but whatever it is, I could also sense how Katherine-Jean whispered and didn't want Manerva to hear about anything that would upset her because it was obvious Manerva had fainted from exhaustion. I'm just glad Katherine-Jean was with her, to keep her calm and thank God dad was there to talk to her earlier and Manerva doesn't have to add Katherine-Jean's concern's to all of the other things she is already dealing with. I'm sure he gave her good legal advice and the shoulder she needed because the message he had left me was that all was OK. He said he had transferred all of his calls to his answering service and he was beginning to get excited about Saturday night."*

Deanna had rationalized everything in her mind, so she could stay focused and enjoy her night with her godchildren. She loved every moment she could be with them. Being around Valerie and Brian reminded her of how it was with her and her brother growing up. They seemed to also feel a void in her life after she had found out she may never be able to have any children of her own.

She smiled as she pulled into the parking lot, thinking how right Manerva had been when she told her just after Roman had died and she read the letter he had left me, *"Deanna, don't worry, God knew what was best for you and Roman. Your relationship and love will always live through the love you give to children of others. Children they birth and you love. That is that same love you gave Roman when he couldn't get it from his parents. You will never know how special that love is. You wouldn't be able to give it to all the special children that really need it, if you gave it all to a child from Roman."*

Deanna would just wait in the car for Valerie and Brian...

Later, after Valerie and Brian had gone to sleep Deanna went into her bedroom and got in her bed to go to sleep. *Deanna Karen Sumner* lay back feeling good. She thought back on all that had happened on this cold, snowy day. She could never have imagined how happy she was. She had a wonderful relationship with her mom and dad. She had wonderful friends. Her work was so fulfilling to her. She couldn't explain why she enjoyed what the others she worked with complained so about. She enjoyed all the long hours and hard work she put in. She was financially set in every area of her life she could possibly think of. She had become the person she had always desired to be. She lived by herself but she never felt lonely. Her thoughts now were of loving memories, not of sadness. She knew healing had taken place in her life.

At that moment sitting on the fireplace mantel was a picture in a small white hand painted frame. It seemed to glow from the light of the moon that came from her window. One would never imagine with the rays of light from above that it was cold and snow below. She could see the picture in the frame very clearly. It was a full length photo of a young girl about the age of twelve. She had a long brunette braided ponytail of hair hanging to the front of her chest over her shoulder. You couldn't tell where the braid ended because it blended so well with her dark leotards. She was standing on her tip toes, in a swan-like stance by a dance bar over looking a window. This full length photo captured all of her grace and charm.

Deanna thought, looking into her eyes and saying, *"Now I understand how you could be so gentle yet so powerful."* It took me almost forty years to learn it, but now I know. This was Deanna's grandmother Anna, her father's mother. Everyone said Deanna looked just like her. She had her same beautiful big brownish-black eyes, long curly brunette hair, complexion as creamy as a bowl of vanilla ice cream which gave her a look of always having a natural tan. Deanna's parents together had a mixture of Italian, Swedish, Irish, and Asian descent. Her family background was all hard working professionals.

Dr. Sumner would always tell Deanna and her brother Toney, "You both are so much like your grandmother, Anna. She had a mind of her own."

Deanna remembers how her brother use to love to hear their father tell the story over dinner of how Anna rebelliously started to dance. Deanna had seen in Manerva's eyes when she first heard the story, she understood also.

As the story went, according to Dr. Sumner...

"Anna was about eight years old. Her parents wanted her to become the first classical concert pianist in the family. They had arranged for Anna to take private lessons from one of the best piano teachers around. Sometimes at dinner when the subject came up, Anna was expected to respond," as he told the story...

She would look them both in the eye and in a very sweet manner would say, "Mama, papa I want to dance. I don't want to have to sit and play the piano."

Each time she would say that, each time her father would seem to grow angrier, her mother would just look silently with eyes watery, when each time he would say, "No, Anna! Absolutely not! You will do as you are told and that's that."

And each time, Anna would look at her mother and say, "Don't be sad, mama, I will obey, I will learn to play the piano. Then and after a brief pause, she would always say, "I will learn to dance also, you will see."

Her father would become so angry, he would then slam his cup on the table and wipe his bread and say, "Anna, you are excused, go to your room."

Each time, Anna would, get up as sweetly as she had sat down, and say, "Don't be upset papa, I will always obey you. Good night".

She would always, go to her room, say her prayers and go to bed.

Unknowingly, one evening after Anna finished her writing assignment from the blackboard at her school, heading home so she wouldn't be late for her piano lesson; she stopped in the hallway because she heard music coming from the music room across the hall. The other children had left about five minutes ahead of Anna. She walked closer to the door and looked in. She didn't recognize her, but she danced beautifully. The young lady that was dancing noticed Anna looking in and immediately stopped and went to turn the music off. Anna noticed, as she walked toward her, her sweater fell to the floor and she noticed her right arm didn't move at all.

"Hello, I didn't know anyone was still in the building," the young lady said. "Sometimes I like to just dance before I start cleaning, so sometimes I get here early."

"Are you a dancer? asked Anna.

"I use to be but I got real sick and now my right arm doesn't move. Do you like to dance?" she asked.

"I want to be and I will be a great ballet dancer one day, but my father wants me to be a concert pianist," said Anna.

"Maybe, someday I will come and see you as a great ballet dancer! The lady said as she smiled. "May I ask what is the name of the great ballet dancer?"

"Yes, my name is Anna and I've got to go."

"Nice to meet you Anna, I'm Victoria, I hope I see you again," said Victoria.

Occasionally, Anna would hear the music playing and sometimes she went in and sometimes she just looked through the door. Victoria could feel she was looking many times, and unless Anna acknowledged she was there, Victoria would just pretend she was talking out loud to herself. She knew Anna was listening. *Anna had a plan.* She didn't want to disobey her father, so she would just remember everything that she heard Victoria say and do, and every moment she was alone in her own room at home she would practice.

She pretended she danced like Victoria, and when she would see herself in her mirror, she would say, *"See Victoria, your right arm still works."* Anna, kept her word, she would still practice and play the piano for her parents, and she word dance and be happy for herself. This went on for about a year. Victoria, had figured out Anna was learning from her and sometimes when she wasn't there the exact time, she would peek through the keyhole and see Anna dancing in the room. Anna was good. She learned beautifully. Victoria was proud of Anna.

The night of the schools big Music Production, everyone was to perform. Anna's parents were there with all of their friends to hear Anna play the piano in public for the first time. Anna did great playing her music number. Her parents and friends were so proud they stood up and clapped! Toward the end of the production was to be a ballet performance by one of the other students. When the song started playing Anna looked up in total amazement. It was her favorite song, the song that Victoria had danced so well to, the song that she had learned to dance so well to. The song played all the way through and there was no one dancing on the stage, everyone was anxiously awaiting but no one came.

As the head of the school was about to announce on the stage, that there would be no dance performance, Victoria was behind the curtains on stage and called him over. She briefly whispered something in his ear and he returned to the stage and said, "Tonight by special request of

Victoria De Luccinie, the renowned ballet dancer, would like for this song to be played again, and at her request she would like for each of you to just listen and imagine her performing on stage as she danced and was once labeled The *Dancing Swan*!

The music began to play again...

Halfway through Anna opened her eyes and stared right into Victoria's. Victoria walked out on stage as her left arm was stretched out toward Anna. *Effortless, Anna stood up and walked toward Victoria.* In an unknown moment of silence Victoria had disappeared from the stage and Anna was dancing, both arms reaching up high, shoes off, toes pointed, all in the audience was standing in amazement, including Anna's parents.

Anna became known that night as *The Little Dancing Swan.* After the performance, it was Anna's father that dropped to his knees as Anna was coming from the stage. He grabbed Anna and hugged her and wouldn't let her speak. Anna's mother just stood back with tears in her eyes, as if in disbelief that she would ever have seen this day.

"The audience was standing, saying more, more as they turned away waving and smiling at Victoria," end of story Dr. Sumner would always say. Tears would be rolling down everyone's face just as they were now with Deanna.

Chapter Nine

Roberta ! Roberta!

Both she and her brother Toney had their grandmother's looks, and they had her spirit, her fire! The kind of fire to make things happen! To be risk takers! Deanna smiled again, because she saw that same spirit in Valerie.

She had grown through the years to open up to Valerie. She talked to her about her desires and dreams.

Valerie told Deanna tonight, "Aunt Deanna, I admire you so! I want to be just like you when I grow up. I want to be a doctor and work with children just like you but dad wants me to work with him so one day I can take over his business." *Valerie had touched Deanna's heart.* Manerva was so right. Roman would be proud. Katherine-Jean was so happy because she was sensing Valerie was growing up and away from her and she was glad she had turned to Deanna and that Deanna was there for her.

Deanna had shared with Valerie tonight, "Roman and I almost moved to Paris."

Valerie had asked, "Aunt Deanna have you ever wanted to live anywhere other than Chicago? Valerie asked again.

Deanna continued telling Valerie the story, *"So many times how she wondered herself how her life would have been had she and Roman chose to stay in Paris. She would think back often.*

We had been dating for five years. My brother introduced us. Roman was Toney's best friend. We lived almost next door. Toney use to joke about him being the *poor little rich kid.* His parents were divorced. Neither worked, they just went their separate ways traveling. Roman tried so hard to get them to come together. He wasn't trying to get them back together as husband and wife; he just wanted them to just be in the same room together to look like a family.

His biggest wish was for them to come home and have dinner and be a family even if it was just for show and even if it was just on holidays. They had promised him they would be home for sure one Thanksgiving. Roman was so happy, he wanted to cook the dinner himself, so he took cooking classes. My mom had given him her recipe for the sticky rice and Duck. Manerva had showed him how to make a southern sweet potato pie and macaroni and cheese. Manerva's neighbor's husband Dr. V. Parks was a retired doctor and a gourmet chef. He taught Roman a lot. Roman was so impressed with him. Roman sort of became the son he never had. Roman was so happy he had invited everybody over. He had cooked so much food, and he wanted people to have dishes they had never had before. He even had rooms prepared to stay over as long as you wanted to stay. He just wanted his family together.

Everybody came except his parents...

They each called at the last minute and gave excuses of how they couldn't get away. Roman was so hurt, he was really never the same. We decided to go on a vacation to Paris. For one month we had a ball. Roman wanted us to get married there in Paris under the *Eiffel Tower.* He didn't want to come back. We both fell in love with Paris. I found the perfect hospital that I could work at and start my dream of starting my own pediatric clinic. It was in the same area that Roman wanted to open his first chain of restaurants. He even wanted to enroll in a culinary school there.

We had discussed it and he asked me what did I really want to do? He knew my family was in Chicago but my heart was with him. *Until I really grew to understand the spirit my grandmother Anna,* I couldn't be a risk taker, basically I got scared and wanted my comfort zone, so I told him I wanted to go back and wait at least six months to see if I still felt the same way. He loved me and would have done anything for me, so he told me he could wait six months because he was confident that we would still feel the same way later in six months.

He said this would give him time to get all his business plans in order. After we arrived back in Chicago, he drove me home from the airport. *That was the last time I ever saw him.*

I got a call a couple of hours later from the hospital, asking me to come down to identify his body. The wrecker's had just pulled a car out of Lake Michigan. Witnesses later said they had seen a convertible jaguar speeding as if it was headed straight for the lake. Over the years, with the love and support of her family, friends and therapist I've been able to let go of the guilt of still blaming myself.

He had given me a gift while we were in Paris and he had made me promise not to open it until I was back at home in Chicago and I was safe in my bed. I finally got the strength to open it and in it was a set of wedding rings and a letter. I read the letter so many times I have it almost memorized," said Deanna to Valerie.

My Dearest Deanna,

If you are reading this letter, and you kept your promise, you are in Chicago and safe in your bed! I love you! You belong with your family in Chicago. I ask for forgiveness for even asking you to move away from something I would have given anything to have, your family. Please know, Paris was for me, not you, but there is no way I could have lived there without you. I have always loved you! There are two things I want you to do.

First, here are our rings the day we got married standing under the Eiffel Tower. The day the angels from heaven came down and slipped them on our fingers. That was the day you made me the happiest man alive! You saved me in so many ways. You were my friend, sister, brother, mother, father, lover and lastly wife. You left not knowing you are a married lady. So, Mrs. Roman LaMonet, I want you to take these rings and go on with your life. Don't look back, only look ahead. That month was my lifetime with you.

Also, contact my lawyer, I have made sure all of my papers are in order and I leave everything I own to you, my wife, Mrs. Deanna LaMonet. You gave me the only real thing I ever needed and that was your love. If you ever need more, it is in the papers, you have ownership of everything my mother and father have also. They could never give me their love, so they gave me controlling shares of their money. You are my family!

Secondly, please use this check for whatever you choose to. I just want you happy! Please make sure your mother and father read this letter. Please help them understand, I can do more for you away than I could there. Be strong Deanna for them. Thank them for loving me like a son. Tell them Toney made me promise until the day I die not to say anything; I have kept my promise until now. Tell your mom and dad Toney loved them and for them not to continue blaming themselves, they were always there for you and him. He left them an unopened letter I'm placing in this box also from him. Deanna Toney wanted me to tell you not to grief him any longer either because he is happy. He found someone who genuinely loved him and he said as long as they are together he is happy. Tell your parents I loved them.

Here is the deed on a house I bought for you. It is around the corner from your parents. If you want to sell it or give it away, that's okay by me. This is the house I saw and wished we lived in if I was there. Please tell our friends I loved them. Please help them financially if needed. Remember Deanna, having money and riches are no good unless you can share it with people you love .You may see my mother and father at my funeral. If they come, let them know I love them, and I forgive them.

Deanna, if you ever need me, just come to bed and talk to me, I'll hear you.

Good Night,
From Your Husband Roman LaMonet
"Andrew, I think you better slow down...

Or Manerva will have to come and get us out of jail," said Emma. "You are over the speed limit and you know the cops don't play with us driving this brand new Cadillac from the south and speeding."

"Emma, how many times do I have I got to tell you things have changed, and remember I have my honorary deputy's badge, just in case I'm stopped," Andrew said.

"Just slow down, we haven't seen our baby girl, since she came home last Christmas, I can't wait to surprise her," Emma said.

"Yeah, you are right, I can't wait to see the look on my big girl's face, when she sees us. The whole church sends their love; they even sent her a plaque. That Dr. Sumner is a real nice man. He said she has no idea, she thinks he is the one that will be honored! The joke is surely going to be on our Manerva!" smiling as he said that.

"Our Manerva, a big time lawyer, here in Chicago, who would have thought it, especially after she left medical school. I'm just glad she's happy, and I think Michael is ready to settle down. Her friend Deanna said she doesn't even know he will be there and the guest speaker. All these years and he never married either. That was so nice of him to offer to fly us to Chicago with him," said Emma.

"You will never get me on an airplane, anyway I needed to blow this car out on the highway," he said grinning and driving.

"Andrew, you haven't changed since the day I married you thirty seven years ago with that old pick up ford truck. God has been good to us, a beautiful daughter, good health and strength, what more could we ask for?" Emma said.

"Then, I better slow down, because I preached that sermon last Sunday on how men need to listen to their wives more, got to practice what I preach. We should get to Chicago in about three hours if I drive the speed limit. Thank God they salt the streets because the weatherman said they got up to six inches of snow late last night," Andrew said as he looked over at Emma .

"Manerva's old medical school friend Alison and her husband, called before we left and told me they were driving up also, they are leaving out of Memphis early Friday morning. You can tell Manerva's friend Deanna is loaded with money, because she insisted on paying for everybody to stay at one of those expensive bed and breakfast hotel suites in downtown Chicago. She said it's in the most expensive areas' in Chicago called the *Magnificent Mile* where all the *Big Shots* hang out! She also said it's within walking distance of the law firm and hospital our baby girl works at and just a few miles from where our baby girl lives also. I'm so glad she has such wonderful friends and people in her life. Deanna said she and our baby girl are both god mothers to another nurse friend's children. Seems like they are all good people. I have all their cellular numbers also," said Emma.

"Emma, you talk about her friends being loaded and rich, look at her parents!" Andrew said.

"Andrew, we got just a little more than the twenty dollars we had when we got married thirty seven years ago!" Emma said smiling.

"Woman, how many times, I got to remind you that we are rich, because our father is rich, with many mansions, don't get me started. Do you mean the guess who is coming to dinner couple?" asked Andrew.

"Now, Andrew, that's not nice," said Emma.

"They are a very nice couple, but Emma, you know I'm telling the truth. I'm just glad Manerva had us all to meet at the rehearsal dinner and before the wedding. You can sure tell they are rich, I don't think they had ever imagined so many blacks at their daughter's wedding. I mean, I did the ceremony, our baby girl was the maid of honor, and the groom black, after it was all over with them both seemed happy for their daughter but you could tell they were still in a state of shock," Andrew said. "I have talked up an appetite; do we have any more of that chocolate cake left?"

"Yes, I packed plenty, because if we stop to eat we will loose time and I'm ready to see my baby girl," Emma said placing pieces of cake in Andrew's month. "Keep watching the road, shut up and open up! Now chew Andrew, chew and watch the road!" said Emma, placing bite after bite and fussing.

Deanna could hear also...

While gazing in the moonlight next to Anna's picture her favorite red, white and black geisha porcelain clock that chimed the most soothing music on the hour, she heard it in the background and knew it was nine o'clock. Her mother had given her this clock. She had gotten it from her homeland before she left Japan. It had been one of the few artifacts her mother had kept to remind her of her roots.

Just as Deanna, was about to close her eyes and go into a peaceful sleep, she was awakened by more sound, this time it was a soft ring of her telephone. She immediately picked it up, not even looking at the caller ID. For the first moment she didn't recognize the male voice, and then she recognized it was Kenneth.

"Hello, may I speak with Deanna Sumner," he said.

"This is Deanna," she said.

"Hi Deanna, this is Manerva's friend Kenneth, my apologies for calling you so late but I'm stuck in a situation that may not be much better in the next day or so. Since I had the time now, I figured why not let you know so you can make other arrangements. I don't think I will be back on Saturday for the award dinner. In fact, I am still in the airport here in New York. They have stopped all flights coming in or going out," he said.

"Oh my goodness, are you alright?" she asked.

"Yes, I'm fine," he said.

"Kenneth, I'm glad you are alright and sorry to hear you may not be able to make it, I know Manerva would want you safe more than anything," said Deanna.

"It is a mad house here; everyone is still just sitting or sleeping while we're waiting here. All of the surrounding hotels are full that are within walking distance, and the police are encouraging everyone to just stay in because of the weather. There is ten inches of snow now and they are expecting six more inches by morning. The weathermen had forecasted only a light snow dusting for last night. The whole city is almost at a standstill. They have some food here and are trying to make sure everyone is as comfortable as possible inside. I'll call you back tomorrow to keep you posted if I can. I wanted to let you know for sure, if you need to have someone else take and present the dozen roses to Manerva on her big night day after tomorrow. I hate I may not make it," said Kenneth.

"This is a situation, you don't have any control over, you just take care of yourself, I appreciate you letting me know in advance," said Deanna.

"I haven't talked to Manerva since last night; both our schedules have been so busy. I've been trying to call her all evening. Let me try to call her back now, maybe she has gotten home," said Kenneth.

Deanne's thoughts went running in head rapidly, "I'd better not mention Katherine-Jean having Manerva go to the hospital to have test run, after she fainted, or that would make things more difficult for him. He has enough things to worry about for now. There would be nothing he could do if he knew. Plus, it would be additional worry for Manerva if she knew his situation. No, I'd better not mention anything more. I know Katherine-Jean will either screen her calls if they are back at Manerva's or let the answering machine pick up. If there had been any type of problem she would have called me back," she thought.

"Kenneth, you take care of yourself, and keep me posted on all," she said.

"I will, thanks, Oh! Here is the telephone number here in the airport that I can be paged from, in case my charge is gone on my cellular phone," said Kenneth.

Chapter Ten

Wake Up Manerva!

Meanwhile, at the hospital...

Katherine-Jean didn't know what to do. Everybody was still waiting on all of the test results to come back. She was told Manerva was still unconscious but stable. Being a nurse herself, she knew exactly what that meant. She also knew what they were not saying also! Both Manerva's neighbors were there. Dr. Rhonda Parks was already there working on some late cases being one of the hospital's medical examiners. Her husband Dr. Vernon Parks had come to pick her up and they stop by one of his restaurants for a late dinner. He was also a retired surgeon and still served on the board of trustees. Both were in consulting with the emergency room physician staff.

Katherine-Jean had tried calling Manerva's parents once the ambulance arrived at the hospital. She had gotten the answering machine. She knew they were driving and on their way there. With all that had gone on in her life she had remembered to call them first thing when she had returned home from her trip. They were so excited about their baby girls' big surprise night in less than two days. Katherine-Jean was thinking aloud, *"Thank goodness Deanna had gotten them a beautiful bed and breakfast suite just a block away from the hospital. They weren't exactly sure what time they would arrive in Chicago, and didn't want to get Manerva too suspicious of arriving too soon. Manerva had invited them and they had told her they would try to get there sometime on Friday but told her they really wasn't sure what time they would arrive? Manerva had told them anytime they got in was fine, she had gotten her guest bedroom ready. Manerva told them she would just be too glad to see them. It didn't matter how late to just come. When they had found out from Deanna the entire affair was for Manerva, they had decided to get in earlier to help and make sure they were here," said Katherine-Jean.*

She looked at her watch then and thought they should be arriving within a couple of hours. She would try to call the hotel to she if they had arrived. No need to have them or Deanna upset just yet. She knew she would have to tell them all as soon as possible, she just wasn't sure how soon.

Katherine-Jean knew everyone that Manerva loved and that was important to her was enroute or headed her way for her big surprise night anyway. Her parents would be two blocks away. The person we all knew she had loved for years but life has kept them apart would be the guest speaker and be in the same hotel as her parents. Her friends from medical school would be staying there also. All of her friends and colleagues from the surrounding areas would be at the banquet.

Deanna said she had mentioned to Manerva that Dr. Sumner had invited Michael, when she had told them she had invited her new friend to escort her. Neither Deanna nor Katherine-Jean knew for sure Michael would be able to attend. Neither did they know that Manerva and her new friend were becoming close. Manerva hadn't really talked a lot about him except she wanted to get to know him better because they had just met less than a month ago. They knew her heart was with Michael and maybe she was tired of waiting. Neither knew Michael's plans they only knew they didn't want any problems for Manerva. That's why when they had heard Michael was coming they had to get word to Manerva, so she could make that decision if she still wanted Kenneth to attend.

In fact Manerva had shared that Kenneth had offered to escort her to the banquet when she had mentioned it. Manerva shared she had given Kenneth, Deanna's telephone number to contact her to see if as her escort she needed him to do anything else since she was working with the event planner.

Everybody who meant something to Manerva would be here, and everybody is so excited to share in her honor because she is such a beautiful person and has been there for each of us in some special way.

Katherine-Jean was so worried...

And didn't know what to do. Besides blaming herself for telling Manerva all that she had to provoke her condition, she just wanted to do what was right. Katherine-Jean, looking at her dear friend laying as peaceful as ever said as she bent down and kissed her forehead, *"Manerva please wake up!"*

Talking so Manerva could hear the strength in her voice and not see or realize the tears rolling down her face said, "You know you are much better at this than me, but I know if it were me lying where you are you be saying a lot of things to God. I don't have the hook up with God that you have. And let me get *the book* I see on the other side on the shelf. Well, at this point I don't know how God is really feeling about me. But if what you've always told me about him never judging you and always hearing you then, I know he will hear me now for you. *I remember you always telling me no matter what you were going through when you said the twenty third Psalm from the book, you know I mean the bible God worked miracles. I know God listens especially through you and when the book is near. I remember you saying it twice and God stepped in and worked miracles.*

The first was when you and I were in Deanna's room with her after Roman had died. A part of Deanna wanted to die and it was your prayer that we all know gave her the strength to open the gift he had given her. I remember how we all looked and felt when the rings fell out and she read the letter Roman had written to her. It was then she miraculously had the strength and spirit to go on. She became a different person at that moment and was able to go down and identify his body and do what was needed to be done. The three of us knew that strength came only from God.

The second time was, when I told you that I knew Donald had been cheating on me. I remember telling you I had always known deep down for sixteen long years he had been unfaithful. I remember telling you I had stopped loving him twelve years ago. I remember telling you I had become pregnant and was unfaithful and I wasn't sure if Donald was the father. We had blood test run and found out that Donald was the father. Donald had threatened me then with getting a divorce and taking custody of Valerie and saying I was an unfit mother. He didn't go through with it and shortly afterwards was when his company was going bankrupt.

We are only together now because I never left and took the children. I met you and the Sumner about this time. The love I had for Donald has long been gone. I didn't have the strength to fight him then because he threatened to tell the children. He threatened he would tell Valerie I wasn't her real mother and Brian I was an unfit mother and take their money. For Donald it has always been about the money. He had nothing when I met him. All of the money came from my parents. They placed the money in trust funds for each of my children. So, if he remains their father prior to them turning eighteen he keeps control of their money. Donald wants the divorce now because he knows Valerie will turn eighteen in less than two years.

Manerva, I remember like it was yesterday, you praying and saying the twenty third psalm and asking God to give me the strength to do the right thing. You asked that for me not even knowing all of what I just told you that I had been going through. It was almost immediately then, my thoughts and feelings changed. I knew strongly that it was not about me it was all about my children. I can't explain it. It was like all of the fear and things I had been thinking really didn't matter.

All I knew was that it was from God. It was as though, I became a totally different person living to do whatever I had to do to keep them safe and from Donald. I knew then that God had placed you and the Sumner Family in my life for a very special reason. What I'm saying now Lord is I know I've sinned big time and I'm not Manerva and I can't pray like Manerva, but I'm asking from the bottom of my heart to help her, please lord help my friend. Lord, I have the book in my hand and if you could listen to me like you do Manerva and work through me today because I don't know anything else to do and I know you can do it, please help Manerva." said Katherine-Jean.

Dear God, whatever your will is for my beloved friend, if you can work out another miracle for her, I'm asking you to please do it so she can wake up. Well, lord it's really the only one I know by heart and I know it's Manerva's favorite and if you hear me, then I'm asking for her as she has so many times for others. Please let her wake up. Let her be alright. Dear God, you can make it happen. Manerva use to always tell me when she said it, it became alive inside her. All I know is,

> *The Lord is my shepherd; I shall not want. He maketh me to lie down In green pastures: he leadeth me beside the still waters. He restored my soul: he leadeth me in the paths of righteousness for his name's sake. Yea, though I walk through the valley of the shadow of death,*
>
> *I will fear no evil: for thou art with me; thy rod and thy staff they comfort me. Thou preparest a table before me in the presence of mine enemies: thou anointest my head with oil; my cup runneth over. Surely goodness and mercy shall follow me all the days of my life: and I will dwell in the house of the Lord for ever. Amen*

With her eyes still closed, and almost in the middle of Katherine-Jean saying the twenty third psalm, she felt an arm lay on her shoulder as she tightened her hold of Manerva's shoulder. After she finished there was a brief moment of silence because she couldn't move or say anything.

When Katherine-Jean did open her eyes, to her surprise was a room filled with all of Manerva's physicians that had been consulting including Dr. Rhonda Parks and her husband. There were six physicians standing around Manerva's bed. *Each had chosen to join in and had their heads bowed in prayer with Katherine-Jean. She knew God was in the room. She knew Manerva felt and heard everything. She knew Manerva would be alright.* Each of the physicians examined Manerva.

Afterwards, they quietly left her room and beckoned for Katherine-Jean to step outside the door. "We understand you being a nurse realize how uncertain Ms. Jones condition is right now," the attending staff physician said to Katherine-Jean.

"Even though we have run many tests and have the results in, the bottom line is it is still too early to say. She is so very fortunate that you were there to monitor and assist when it happened. According to all the test, they show Ms. Jones suffered severe head injuries due to the sudden and abrupt fall. All of the EEG, CT, and MRI tests indicate some partial seizures did occur. We can not be exactly sure because the spells lasted for only a few seconds. We have medicines to treat these seizures, however at some point Ms. Jones condition triggered a stroke which has brought on her unconsciousness. We don't want to start any drug treatment too soon without knowing the exact cause of the sudden loss of unconsciousness or moments of fainting or seizures. At this point, she is stable and we are hoping she regains consciousness. She is breathing and functioning on her own. We won't know if her functions such as memory loss, sight, speech, movement have been affected until she is conscious. We suggest you contact her family to let them know. We will keep her here for awhile and monitor her closely."

At that moment Katherine-Jean went over to a chair in the waiting area and put her head down and started crying, Dr. Rhonda Parks followed her and sat beside her and said, "Katherine-Jean, we both know how strong Manerva is and we both know she can wake up and everything be alright."

"We both know she could never wake up also! Or she could wake up and be blind or can't move! It's all my fault!" said Katherine-Jean.

"Where is the faith you had just a minute ago in her room? Did it just disappear? We need to be strong and stay positive and hopeful because there is hope. We have seen too many cases like this and things have worked out just fine," said Dr. Parks.

Katherine-Jean looked up and wiped the tears from her eyes and said, "You are right! Manerva will be alright! I need to contact her parents and let Deanna and Dr. Sumner know what has happened.

She looked down at her watch and saw the time was ten o'clock...

" I know it's late but I would want to know, I've got to let them know," said Katherine-Jean.

"Give me their numbers, I'll call them for you, you need to rest and go in and be with Manerva," Dr. Parks said.

"Thanks Doc, I'm fine, this is something I must do! Would you go in and stay with Manerva, I'm going to go over to the waiting area and make some calls," she said.

"Sure. Honey, let's go in and sit with Manerva awhile," Dr. Parks said as she looked up toward her husband standing near.

Katherine-Jean reached down in her pocket and got the list of telephone numbers. She had placed them in her pocket while all of the physicians were examining her. *I wonder have they arrived in Chicago yet. Anyway, they need to know,"* Katherine-Jean sat as she dialed the number not knowing what she would say.

"Hello"

"Hello, who is this," said Andrew.

"Sir, I'm a friend of your daughter Manerva and our other friend Deanna told me you were driving in tonight. Your hotel rooms are just around the corner from where I am now. Knowing your trip is a surprise to Manerva, I wanted to see how far you were especially with our weather outside," Katherine-Jean said while thinking fast.

"Oh, that is so nice of you; we just arrived in our hotel room about ten minutes ago. We were going to go and see our baby girl first, but we passed the downtown area first. With the weather outside, we decided to get settled in first. Manerva had told us it was better to just catch a cab and we didn't have to worry about parking especially between where she lives and this downtown area. So we decided we would do that or if she had already gone to bed we would just wait until morning.

Your other friend Deanna had gotten us this real nice room and told us where ever we wanted to go just pick up the telephone and tell them and they would have a courtesy car pick us up out front and take us. We are waiting for the nice young man to park our car and bring all our luggage up when you called. What is your name?" he asked.

"I'm Katherine-Jean," she said.

"You are the nurse friend with the children," he said. Just then Emma said Andrew give me the phone. She may be able to tell us about our baby girl and you are doing all that talking.

"Hello, Katherine-Jean, I'm Manerva's mother. Do you know if she has gone to bed already? She is expecting us sometime tomorrow. We are so excited and can't wait," said Emma.

"Mrs. Jones, that's the real reason I called you. Please try to stay calm. I am with Manerva now. She is stable and is in the hospital about two blocks from you. If you and your husband would just go back downstairs and tell the courtesy car to bring you to the emergency room at NorthCentral Hospital.

I will tell you all the details then," said Katherine-Jean.

You will be here in five minutes...

"Oh my God! The hospital, our baby girl is in the hospital! We are on our way!" said Emma hanging up the phone. "Andrew come on, we got to go to the emergency room now!"

"Hello, Deanna, did I wake you," said Katherine-Jean.

"No, what's wrong, I can tell in your voice, Katherine-Jean. I can feel something. Tell me everything," said Deanna.

"I'll go more into details later but Manerva is not doing well. She is unconscious, the doctors have all examined her and all the test show head injuries due to the abrupt fall of seizures and a stroke. She has never gained consciousness. Both her neighbors Dr. Parks and her husband have been here with me and all of the physicians. I just called Manerva's parents they had just made it to the hotel and they are on their way," Katherine-Jean said.

"I'm on my way, dad doesn't know or he would have called me. Did you want me to bring the children or I can leave them with my mom?" asked Deanna.

"I know it's late, but I need to see both my children. I think they need to see Manerva also. The doctor's all say they just don't know. I've been praying the twenty third psalm asking God to please let Manerva wake up. Oh, Deanna, it's all my fault. I should not have told Manerva all that I did. She had enough already on her," Katherine-Jean said.

"Stop it! Just stop it! We both know Manerva would have wanted to know exactly all that you told her! And we both know she will be alright, she will pull through this! That's what she would say to us. Now it' our time to be there for her! We are on our way!" Deanna said.

"Drive careful."

"We will."

"Hello, Dad, sorry to wake you but Manerva is in the emergency room. Katherine-Jean just called me, apparently, they were out talking, she fell, had head injuries, seizures and a stroke, she has never gained consciousness. Her parents had just made it into Chicago; they are on their way from the hotel now. I have both Katherine-Jeans children with me. We are on our way to the hospital now."

"Stop by and I'll drive us. Me and your mom want to go. Don't worry about us. We went to bed early, we both have had a couple of hours of sleep already," he said. "My car is bigger and heavier anyway, don't argue."

Michael would want to be there...

"I'll call and tell him. He had left me a message saying he had made it to the hotel about an hour ago and was hoping to surprise Manerva and meet her for breakfast in the morning. Also, let me check with my answering service. I had told them to route all of my calls to my answering service so the on-call staff physician could get them."

"Hello, we are Mr. and Mrs. Jones, and we want to see our daughter *Manerva Ruthie Jones*. We were told she was here," said Emma.

"Yes, she is in room number one. Let me buzz you in, then go to the end of this hall and turn right," the lady sitting at the desk said.

"Thank You," both Emma and Andrew said together.

As they turned the corner, they both saw the number one at the top of the door with the curtains pulled around the bed. Andrew grabbed Emma's hand and they both walked in. Emma slowly pulled the curtain back and quickly held her hand to her mouth to keep from screaming. Andrew held her closely. They both were in shock for a moment. Just to see their baby girl just lying on the bed and not moving. Emma couldn't hold back the tears seeing her doll baby hooked up with IV's going on both her arms. Except the clicking and ticking of machines there was a silence in the air. Andrew reached in his pocket and pulled out his handkerchief. This was the last one in the package Manerva had given him for his birthday.

That was their special bond; he wouldn't use a handkerchief unless Manerva had bought it. She always told him, "Dad, I love it that you are not afraid to show your emotions. I love to see you cry. It's not a sign of weakness but of strong emotions." This was one of those times Andrew, couldn't hold back.

Emma just bent over and started kissing her face. It seemed like the more she kissed the stronger she became and then she was able to speak, "Dollbaby, you listen to your mama. I don't know what happened and I don't care what happened. I just know you are going to be just fine. God just got you resting for a minute, cause you tired. I listen when you tell me about all the different things you been working on. You just that kind of person. You have always been like that. Stubborn like your daddy. Never will stop. And that's good, cause people like you are not meant to stop, that's why he gave you those two hearts, remember. I remember all our little talks about them. In fact I was thinking about that today while we were driving up here. You thought it was for love. What I never told you was they were for something far more special than that.

You see, God had it all worked out, that when one got really, really tired the other one would always be working in the background. No one would ever know it but him. And when he felt you had enough rest. Then, the one everyone else saw including all these fancy doctors could get back to working full force. So, Dollbaby, we will just wait right here until you get your rest back. God didn't bring you or us thus far for nothing. You remember that. I know you hear me. I love You.

You have some wonderful friends. Everybody is excited about the banquet on Saturday night. So get your rest. You know where your daddy is and you know what he is doing. All that big mouth and talk, and when he has his chance to really talk to you, where is he. He got to sit over there and pull one of your handkerchiefs out. You got to buy him some more too. I think that's his last package. Don't worry, you'll hear from him soon enough. I'm going to let him tell you about his new car, and how crazy he was driving up here. Almost got us arrested. And you know him and his honorary deputy badge. We are going to be right outside your door, I think the nurse just came in to get you all cleaned up," Emma said with a sweet smile.

As Emma and Andrew were leaving the room...

They noticed a young lady standing against the opposite wall. The two nurses taking care of their baby girl had called her nurse but she didn't have on a nurse's uniform. As she walked out behind them, Emma turned around, "Are you Katherine-Jean, my doll baby's friend?" she said.

"Yes ma'am, how did you know?" Katherine-Jean asked.

"You just seem like someone special to her. We want to thank you for letting us know," said Emma.

"That is the least, I could do, your daughter has been there for me and others so much. I was telling her about all my problems when she fainted this evening," said Katherine-Jean.

"Don't you dare blame yourself young lady, we don't, our daughter don't and God don't. Didn't you hear my wife talking to our baby girl, she is special in that way always has been and always will be. Telling her your problems, didn't get her like this, God just want her to rest. God just talked through my wife, cause she hit it right on the nose. Our baby girl will be fine. No matter what the doctors say. We are not in denial. We just know our daughter. She is a fighter. Got it from both of us!" said Andrew smiling.

"Hello, you must be Mr. and Mrs. Jones; we are neighbors and friends of your daughter and just happen to both be doctors here also. We just love her. She is great! She is always telling us stories about her family and growing up. I'm Rhonda and this is my husband Vernon," she said. "I am one of the medical examiners on staff here; I work with your daughter on a lot of cases here. I was in several meetings with her today. Everything has happened so fast. Why don't both of you have a seat. The other physicians working with your daughter will be over shortly. I told them I was a friend of the family, and I wanted to introduce myself to you first," explained Dr. Parks.

Just as Andrew and Emma were about to sit down...

They heard a familiar male voice in the background, "Mr. and Mrs. Jones, how is Manerva? I came as soon as I heard? Will they let me in to see her? said Michael grabbing them both to give them a hug.

"We haven't talked to all her doctor's yet to get all the details, we just got here moments ago and rushed right in, these are her doctor friends and neighbors, Mr. and Mrs. Parks," said Andrew. "She is unconscious but we just thank God she is alive. We know she will be alright."

"She is in room one Michael, I'm sure you can go in, they just came out from cleaning her up. We are so glad you are here. I know our baby girl will be glad to know you are here. Just go in and talk to her, I know she will be able to hear you," Emma said.

Coming inside the emergency room...

"Is Aunt Manerva going to be alright, Dr. Sumner? asked Brian, as they were getting out of the car in front of the emergency room driveway.

"We all hope she will be son. She's got some of the best doctors around. I was listening to all their reports through my headsets as I was driving," Dr. Sumner said. "Her condition is stable right now, meaning everything is working just the way they are suppose to work. Your mom took good care of her and got her to the hospital in good time. When you call her name or touch her she will not talk back or move now. We are all hoping she will soon," he further explained.

"You know Dr. Sumner, I've been thinking about it a lot. I know my dad want me to be a business man like him, and at first I did, but now I think I want to be a nurse or a doctor, so I can help people too. Can a man be a nurse?" asked Brian.

"Of course they can Brian, I've worked with a lot of male nurses as well as females like your mom," said Mrs. Sumner. "Brian Mrs. Sumner is a nurse just like your mom also, Dr. Sumner said.

"Honey, why don't you and Deanna go on back. Brian, Dr. Sumner and your Aunt Deanna are both doctors. They can go and see if Aunt Manerva's doctors need any help. I'll wait in here with the Brian and Valerie. We have the TV, some books, and canteen machines all here. We will be fine. You two go!" Mrs. Sumner said.

"Here are some really neat books and magazines," said Valerie.

"I want me a Snapple Orange drink out of the machines," said Brian.

"I'm still full from all that pizza earlier," said Valerie.

"I would like a hot cup of tea," said Mrs. Sumner.

"Well, we can just all walk down to the cafeteria, it's down the hall and around the corner," said Katherine-Jean.

"Mom!"

"Mom! We're glad to see you! Aunt Deanna packed you a suitcase along with some things for Aunt Manerva. Can we go and she her?" asked Valerie.

"Yes, but first, I need some hugs and kisses and then we are all go and sit and get Mrs. Sumner her tea. Then I need to sit and you two tell me about the game and all today, said Katherine-Jean.

"That sounds great except, I think I am going to leave you three alone to bond for a few minutes and I am going to go to the nearest nurses' station area and get some of their hot tea and lemon," Mrs. Sumner said while leaving them.

"Mom, is Aunt Manerva going to be alright? Dr. Sumner explained to us, everything is working alright but she doesn't talk or move. What happened to her? asked Valerie.

"I don't want you two to worry about anything, except we are together right now. After we go sit down and we all talk, I'll take you to see Aunt Manerva. I know she would want to see you both. A lot of things have happened today. I want to try to tell you about them," Katherine-Jean said.

"Mom, did you and dad have a fight again? Brian asked.

"Why would you ask that honey?

Katherine-Jean wondered aloud...

"Mom, please! Brian nor I are blind. Our family trip was a real joke! We didn't do anything all together. Usually you guys can at least fake like we are a pretty OK family. But now it was either us with you or us with dad, and now we noticed all of dad's clothes are gone. He hasn't even called once today," said Valerie.

"We haven't been at home, he may have called and left a message at home," Katherine-Jean said.

"Mom, I had the home phone forwarded to my cellular phone, he hasn't called. Plus you had Aunt Deanna to pick us up and go over her house. We love staying with Aunt Deanna, but mom what's going on?" Valerie asked.

"Yeah, mom, we want to know where dad is. Is he coming back home?" Brain asked looking sadly down.

"Here we all are, let's sit at that table over there looking out of the window over looking the snow and I'll tell you," Katherine-Jean said.

Meanwhile at O'Hara Airport...

"Alison, don't worry, this is the airport shuttle bus. It will take us straight to the Hotel. I am just glad you agreed that we should fly rather than drive. I know you enjoy your long rides but getting in Chicago tonight and getting a good night sleep can only help prepare us for spending the entire day with your parents tomorrow," said Bates.

"It just worked out great, because when my parents told me they would be in Wisconsin for a golf tournament on Sunday, less than an hour away from downtown Chicago, I couldn't resist getting here earlier to spend some time with them. After Deanna had gotten our rooms, I told my dad. He already has a reserved suite there, they use when they visit Chicago. Their suite is a penthouse suite. They should already be there. I told them we should arrive before midnight depending on the traffic in Chicago from the airport," Alison said.

"Let me call Deanna before it is too late, and let her know we made it, in case she needs us to help with anything. We can adjust our schedule on tomorrow with my parents."

"I just can't wait to see the look on Manerva's face on her big night! I didn't even tell her for sure if we both could get coverage to be off so soon," Alison said.

"I can't wait to see the look on Manerva's face either!" Bates repeated.

"Hello, hold on a minute," said Deanne.

"Dad, I need to step outside this nurse's station area to take this call. I had all my calls forwarded with everything going on. I didn't want to miss any one."

"Deanna, I'll leave her chart here," said Dr. Sumner. Deanna stepped from behind the nurse's station into a back office to talk.

"Now, I'm back, thanks for holding, this is Deanna Sumner, who am I speaking to? she asked

"Deanna, this is Alison, sorry to call at this hour, but I wanted you to know we are in Chicago.

We are in a shuttle bus from the airport on our way to the hotel now. My parents were close to Chicago this weekend so we came in a day earlier to spend a day with them and offer our assistance if you needed us for anything," said Alison.

"Alison, I'm so glad you called and that you are here," said Deanna. "I was going to call you, once I knew more, but we are all at NorthCentral Hospital about two blocks from the hotel. Manerva was brought in several hours ago. I just got here and haven't gone in to see her yet. All I know is she fainted, and fell with head injuries, her vitals are stable and she has been unconscious since she was brought in," Deanna said.

"Oh No! Not Manerva, I just talked to her last night," Alison said.

"Excuse me driver how far are we from NorthCentral Hospital? Alison asked the shuttle driver.

"Lady, normally, I would say thirty minutes but the drive is slow maybe because of the weather, looks like the cars are backed up because of an accident up ahead. May take close to an hour," said the shuttle bus driver.

"Hello, Deanna…" "I heard Alison…"

"Deanna, as soon as we can get there we are on our way," said Alison. "We are all still in the emergency room monitoring all," Deanna said. After Alison hung up the telephone from Deanna, Bates grabbed both her hands.

"Honey, I could hear, we both know Manerva is strong. I wonder had her parents made it in or not? Well, thank God we are here and we will be there in no time at all. Speaking of parents, we better call your parents and tell them we will be at the hospital," he said.

"You are right, that's why I love you so, you always keep me calm and focused," said Alison.

"That's what husbands are for," said Bates as he put his arms around her.

"Hi Dad, were you two asleep? asked Alison. "No, actually, we just came up from the hotel lounge downstairs. We decided to socialize some. Your mom hasn't come in from the hot tub area. You know how she is. It's open all night," said Alison's dad. "Where are you love birds?"

"Dad, we are in the airport shuttle bus. We were coming to the hotel but we just found out that something happened to Manerva and she is unconscious in the emergency room at NorthCentral Hospital. We are going straight there."

"Honey, I'm so sorry to hear that. I hope she gets better soon. I'm going to go down and tell your mom everything, I'm sure she would want to know and come see you," he said. "OK dad, we are still on the drive stuck in traffic, it may take up to an hour to get there, I'll keep you posted if I know anything further, tell Mom, Bates and I sends our love," she said.

"Its times like this that make me realize how important having you in my life is. I was just talking to Manerva, yesterday and we both were talking about how both our lives have changed so. How both of us quit medical school and have had no regrets. We both felt that it was more important to have been accepted and had the opportunity; than to never have been accepted at all. Back fifteen years ago, we both were there because it was really what our parents wanted for us more than what we wanted for ourselves. It was a time when things were very different. Doors were being opened for more black females to attend predominately white medical schools. As well as white females attending southern medical schools. We talked about how our friendship has always been so unique because we met doing this period of change. I think in a lot of ways, my friendship with Manerva allowed me to not be afraid of realizing how special you were to me," Alison said while lying in bates arms crying.

"After Manerva, left medical school, I took a long hard look at myself and realized I really didn't want to practice medicine, I wanted to teach. So, after the next quarter, I was able to enroll in a teaching program."

"That's when I saw you talking to some of the laboratory instructors," said Bates.

"I loved how you just happened to come and ask to sit with me for lunch a couple of times, Alison said. "Why did it take you five entire years before we let everybody else know we were dating? Alison asked.

"Because that was the south, baby, and I knew it wouldn't be easy for us and especially not until I became a Manager in the Laboratory. I wanted to be able to afford you a little," he said smiling.

"Well, all I know is you have made me very happy. I just want Manerva to be alright too, she deserves so much too," said Alison. "We didn't talk everyday, but through the years we have always kept up with what each other were doing. She has been like a sister to me. I remember how hard she took it when both my godparents that she first stayed with in Chicago died. Even working her jobs she helped them as much as she could. They never had children so they cherished Manerva and me as their own. They left her money so she wouldn't have to work so hard to pay for her schooling. I was glad of that because she would never take money from me. She would always tell me how her parents had raised her that she would only take money she had worked for and earned. My godparents realized this early on and somehow they made Manerva feel she was working for them by taking them to their doctors, picking up their medicines, taking them to church and other everyday things that became hard for them to do themselves," said Alison.

Chapter Eleven

She Is Three Months Pregnant!!!

"Manerva is a real special person for so many people," Bates said. "I remember the night I first met her, was actually fifteen years ago in the emergency room. I had never felt or seen anyone else show the compassion she showed for a patient she had never met before. The patient died and there was never any more talk about it around the hospital. I looked for Manerva for the next couple of days but I was only told she had left medical school. It was something about the whole thing that didn't feel right to me, in fact it became rather spooky. The patient died, Manerva left, no mention of anything, no rumors, so I had nothing to go on, so I let it go. It was only until we started dating and years later that I found out she had been your roommate and suddenly moved to Chicago. Since she never brought it back up, I just thought whatever happened was too personal and none of my business," he said.

"Folks, there is NorthCentral Hospital up ahead, we should be there in ten minutes," the shuttle driver said.

Not knowing where to start...

"Valerie, Brian there is so much to say and I don't know where to begin," said Katherine-Jean.

"Mom, just start at the beginning, said Valerie.

"Alright, but I want both of you to sit closer so I can put my arms around both of you while I'm telling you all this. I always knew this day would come, but I hadn't expected it tonight of all nights and in a hospital cafeteria," Katherine-Jean said.

"Mom!"

"OK, Brian. I want both of you to know I love you both very much. I always have and I always will. Nothing I am going to tell you will ever change that. It all started about sixteen years ago, in a little town in Arkansas. No it actually started way before that, I remember growing up as an only child, and always dreaming and hoping that one day I would have a beautiful family, just like the two of you. *I thank God for both of you everyday.* I remember being an only child and saying how I couldn't wait to have children of my very own and a husband to love so I would no longer feel like I was alone. Most of my school friends would talk about their dreams of traveling and all my dreams were always to have a family to love.

I want you two to know no matter want faults your dad and I may have or any of the problems we may have; that has nothing to do with the love and joy you two have brought in our lives. That is the kind of love a mother would gladly die for if she had to, if it meant saving her children. That is the kind of love only a mother, a real mother, can feel growing down in her womb no matter what she had to endure to have that feeling. That is the kind of love that became one even if it came from two different bodies.

I *need both of you to listen to me with your hearts* because I know it may become difficult as I tell you the love I have for both of you has grown stronger and the love I have for your father has gone away as has his love for me," Katherine-Jean said.

"Mom, are you saying dad no longer loves us? Valerie asked as Brian was attentively listening. "No, I'm saying your dad no longer loves me? Katherine-Jean answered.

"All of the problems are between me and your dad. We have gone through a lot of bad things and a lot of good things too. Look at you two," she said barely smiling.

"Will dad still be living with us, Mom? asked Brian.

"No, your dad will be living somewhere else, I don't know where, and Dr. Sumner and Aunt Manerva when she gets better will be helping me figure out things about when you will see your dad?" said Katherine-Jean.

"Mom, are you and dad getting a divorce?" asked Valerie.

"Yes, we are, and we will all still be fine. It's not going to be easy because you two may hear some things that are not very nice about your dad and me. Just promise me you will always remember how much you are both loved and..."

At that very moment over the cafeteria speakers...

All could hear, *Code Blue Stat in the Emergency Room One*, Respiratory Stat, EKG Stat..."

"We have to go now, Valerie, Brian, just follow me, hurry," said Katherine-Jean as the three of them rushed out of the cafeteria racing down the hallway.

Moments later, pushing pass all of the hospital personnel and machines, Katherine-Jean went in through a side entrance to bypass the nurse's station. As she looked up she saw everyone standing up looking down the hall as vital traffic was continually rushing in and out.

"Valerie, I need you and Brian to stay back here, until I come back and get you, do you understand?

Aunt Manerva is in Room One. I see her parents and all standing just outside her room. When we heard them page code blue, that meant the patient is unresponsive, they are not breathing or their heart has stopped beating. I need to go and see what is happening but I don't want either of you any closer. I'll come back and get you both. Do you understand?"

"Yes Mom, we will stay here, just go help Aunt Manerva," said Valerie. As she was leaving, she saw Mrs. Sumner walking toward her.

"Katherine-Jean, you go, I'll stay with the children. I went looking for you and the children and I heard the page too and came running. Go find out what is going on. I haven't seen my husband or daughter. They must be in the room," she said.

Katherine-Jean, trying to keep her composure but pushing through everyone, looked up and saw Dr. Parks and her husband standing at the end of the hospital bed. She tried to look with tears falling from her eyes but couldn't see the patient's face because the code blue team was all around working. All she could hear was, "stand back," as the team repeated their efforts with the shock treatments.

She looked all around for Manerva's parents but didn't see them. At that moment Katherine-Jean could see Dr. Sumner and Deanna standing behind at the other side of the room. She was crying so hard, she couldn't see them clearly, but she could feel a gentle arm on her shoulder, when she heard, "all clear" from the code blue team.

"We're getting a steady reading now, the pulse is increasing, everybody clear the room," the unfamiliar voice said.

As Katherine-Jean managed to reach over and grab a kleenex tissue from the box on one of the carts, Dr. Parks asked, "We are glad this patient is okay, have you come from Manerva's room, and is there any change with her?"

At that moment with clear open eyes Katherine-Jean looked up and now could she an older lady lying in the bed. "She took the chair, and sit down, you have been through a lot this evening, Mr. Parks said as he pushed the chair closer for her to sit in it.

"I'll be fine, I just need to catch my breath for a minute and get back to my children," said Katherine-Jean.

"No sooner than they moved Manerva down to room three, they brought this new patient in and paged code blue for room one. Manerva's physicians took her parents and friends into the waiting area to talk to them. We came in her to brief Dr. Sumner and Deanna on everything when we saw them, said Dr. Parker.

"Let me go get my children, they are anxious to visit their Aunt Manerva," said Katherine-Jean.

"We all are here Katherine-Jean," said Dr. Sumner.

"We saw her moments before we came in here and all her vitals are still stable. She's fighting to come back to us. I agree with Dr. Parks and all her physicians, to make a move administering certain drugs would not be to Manerva's best interest if there is any chance she will re-gain consciousness on her own. We are monitoring all; giving IV's to make sure her electrolytes and lab work are stable. We are still waiting on a few urine test and we are running blood cultures to make sure there is no infection," he said.

Deanna walked over and put her arms around Katherine-Jean, "You did good, getting her here, and we have to stay strong for Manerva. She's coming back to us. We just need to be there for her," said Deanna. "Let's go get Mom and the children over there, and be with Manerva. We are all her family," Deanna said wiping tears from her eyes and walking.

"Mom, how is Aunt Manerva, we saw everyone in her room?" asked Brian.

"Manerva was moved to another room, so she was not in that room, but that patient is going to be alright, now let's all go and visit Aunt Manerva," Katherine-Jean said as Valerie and Brian each grabbed one of her arms.

As they entered the waiting room all eyes met...

Katherine-Jean walked straight over to Emma.

Emma had stood with her arms wide open and placed them spread eagle around all three.

"You must be Brian and Valerie," Emma said.

"Yes ma'am, I'm Brian and this is my sister Valerie, said Brian.

"My baby girl has told me nothing but good things about both of you," Emma said.

"We don't want her sick, can we go in and tell her how much we love her, and for her to hurry up and be able to talk and move again?" he asked.

"Brian, we have to check with her doctors first," Valerie said.

"I'm sure she would like that very much, said one of Manerva's physicians.

"Hello Mr. and Mrs. Jones, I'm Deanna, I'm sorry with all that just happened in the other room I saw you but hadn't gotten a chance to properly introduce myself. I'll be glad to take the children in, if that's alright with you Katherine-Jean. You've done enough all evening. You just sit and relax," Deanna said.

"If it's okay, when you all come out, we'd like to just take a minute and let her know we are here also, we are her friends from Memphis, Alison and Bates," said Alison to her physician.

"Sure, I don't see a problem with that, I fact at this point, anything could bring her to consciousness. It's her strength and will that could make the difference," her physician said.

"I'm sorry Doc, but I beg the difference, it's the will of God that will make the difference," said Andrew. "And we know it's just a matter of time," said Emma.

"Amen, Pastor," Michael said as he walked over from Manerva's room. "Michael, we are so glad you could come," said Mrs. Sumner. "I am glad to be here. I'm glad we are all here. We all love Manerva," he said looking as Deanna, Valerie and Brian walked into her room.

"Bates, Alison, glad you both made it early, I didn't expect you two until tomorrow," Michael said.

"Neither did we, but we are so happy to see you, Emma said.

"I think you both better have a seat because if you slowly turn around you will see another blessing at the desk," Andrew said smiling.

"Mom, dad, here we are, you both came," Alison called out in excitement as Bates helped her up off the sofa. "God is truly in the blessing business to have all of us from all walks of life be here unexpectedly at midnight with six inches of snow outside. When my baby girl know all this she will wake up, just trust God," Andrew said as he went around and thanked everyone for being here.

Just then two hostesses came into the waiting area with Dr. Parks bringing extra pillows and blankets and announcing fresh coffee or hot tea was in the kitchen area of the waiting room. They also announced that the chairs and sofas let out to make comfortable beds. After everyone had gotten a pillow and blanket to be as comfortable as possible, Bates looked at Alison and she smiled and nodded back at him saying yes.

As the hostesses were about to leave...

Bates stood and said, "We hadn't planned on this tonight, but what better time than now, Ma'am, before you leave, could my wife have a couple of extra pillows just in case, we just found out, *she's three month's pregnant! We're having a baby!"*

For a moment there was a complete silence in the room. Then came a loud, "Praise God!" said Andrew.

"Honey, did you hear that, we are going to be grandparents," Alison's dad said as Alison's mom couldn't stop holding her face as tears of happiness fell from her face.

Everybody got back up hugging and congratulating both Alison and Bates and her mom and dad. That announcement seemed to bring a calm in the waiting room. An unspoken unity came from within also, almost simultaneously, each time one person came from within Manerva's room another person went in. No one left that waiting room. Even the doctors like Dr. Sumner and Dr. Parks or Alison's parents with their plush office or hotel suites within two blocks. No one wanted to leave. Each person that went in would sit with Manerva and talk or just hold her hand anywhere from fifteen minutes to thirty minutes. All of the nurses at the nurse's station were amazed at how systematically everybody did this throughout the night.

Valerie and Brian were the only ones that seemed to sleep straight through.

It was as though everybody else used that waiting time to sort out what they were going to do with the rest of their lives. It was as though each person there knew they were there for a different reason than the one they thought they had come for.

They sectioned themselves in families as much as possible.

Andrew and Emma were on the sofa closest to the door facing Manerva's room. Emma was just lying resting thinking. Andrew was sitting on the end of the sofa next to the table lamp reading his scriptures in his bible.

Chapter Twelve

Who Is Roberta?

Michael had just come from Manerva's room...

As Andrew began to get up to go and Michael sat in the reclining chair adjacent to the table lamp, opened his briefcase and started writing.

Dr. Parks and her husband were on the sofa to the right of Emma and Andrew. Both were just lying back with eyes closed resting.

The Sumner were all together on the opposite side of the room sitting in the three large recliner chairs.

Katherine-Jean was sharing a cart with Valerie next to Brian lying on a sofa near the center of the room.

Alison, Bates, her mom and her dad had all moved to the far side of the room so they wouldn't disturb the others talking. They were discussing different plans for the baby.

Before anyone really realized it Friday morning had arrived...

A continual flow of hospital personnel slowly walked through the waiting room indicating the shift was changing.

Dr. Sumner, Dr. Parks and Deanna each had made their individual visits to Manerva's room and were sitting in the kitchen area drinking their coffee and checking pagers and answering services for messages.

"I feel more rested than I had expected. I was glad to be able to freshen up using the facilities upstairs on the third floor," said Deanna.

Let me tell everyone there are extra scrubs and toothbrushes, soap and other items, even a hair dryer if up there if needed."

"Good morning, that sounds great, Valerie, Brian and I are going up now and come back down to visit with Manerva. We will just take our suitcases you packed and brought," said Katherine-Jean smiling.

"Michael is still in there now, he insisted. The nurse put a recliner in the room next to her bed and he stayed holding her hand all night," Emma explained.

"Things are working out great, I received a message earlier this morning from Manerva's new friend Kenneth stating he is still stuck in New York and that conditions have not gotten any better. There are no flights leaving because of the snow, they have twelve inches now and still expecting more. He is fine and sends his apologies for not being able to make the banquet on tomorrow," Deanna announced.

"Morning all, who is this Kenneth?" asked Andrew.

"Good morning Mr. Jones, Kenneth is a new friend of Manerva's. She had invited him to escort her. She knew nothing of this being a surprise for her nor did she know Michael was coming or going to be the guest speaker. She didn't want to be a successful lawyer attending a gala banquet alone, as she put it," Deanna said smiling.

"Well, she's not alone, Michael is with her and whoever this Kenneth fellow is, I wish him well in all that snow, but he need to just stay where he is in New York," Andrew said while pouring himself a cup of coffee.

"This is a very nice hospital. I'm so pleased my baby girl is getting such good care. And they take care of the visitors as well. A hostess brought in fresh towels and everything we needed this morning to make sure we were okay. They even gave us all free passes for our meals throughout our stay. This type of service sure beats the service given in our hospitals back home," he said.

"Good Morning, I agree totally," said Bates.

"Well, good morning, I see everybody is all up," Alison said.

"Honey, how do you feel, this morning," asked her mom.

"I'm fine mom; I want to know how Manerva is? she asked.

"I just went in and all her doctors are in examining her now, they said she rested well through the night. They still sound hopeful," said Emma.

"Since everyone is here, let's all take a moment and thank God for waking us up this morning and bringing us all together and letting my baby girl have a peaceful night. That is truly a blessing," said Andrew. "Let's all just bow our heads for a moment of prayer and let God hear your hearts."

After a moment of prayer and silence...

Andrew said, "Amen!"

And everyone in the kitchen area said, "Amen!"

At that very moment in total amazement...

Two new hostesses walked in the waiting area pushing several carts with fresh cooked breakfast food buffet style from the cafeteria.

"This is the power of God, I feel like I am sitting on one of those expensive airlines I see on TV, when the airline stewardess goes up and down the aisles and prepares your meal. You never have to even leave your seat. Wait until I tell my church about this service," said Andrew. "Oh, you are all welcome to our church."

" If you think he talks now, you need to hear him preach. Every time he opens his mouth, I never know what is coming out next? Emma said.

"Neither do I," said Andrew.

After everybody found a comfortable place to sit, their breakfast was served, the food was blessed and they all enjoyed a good hot breakfast. Just as everyone was finishing there breakfast, they looked up as all of Manerva's physicians walked into the crowed waiting room area.

Again, silence was in the air...

Everybody looked up, too scared to speak.

Manerva's main physician walked over to Andrew and Emma, placing his hand on Andrew's shoulder and said, *"Good news, Manerva is slowly beginning to show signs of consciousness."*

Everybody quickly started showing signs of happiness and all her physicians smiled. All you could hear in that crowed waiting room area was excitement. Everybody started thanking God and each other and crying tears of happiness.

Her main physician turned around as he walked out of the door and said, "One more thing, it's going to take time for her to re-gain total consciousness, she is slowly showing movement with her entire body, and she keeps calling out the name Roberta, Who is Roberta?" he asked.

"Roberta, that's the name she called me at the time she fainted," said Katherine-Jean.

"She has never mentioned any of her friends to me named Roberta," said Emma.

"Not to me either," said Andrew.

"I only know of one person she told me about named Roberta when we first met years ago," Michael said.

She was a patient who Manerva said had died in surgery one night...

When she was still in medical school," said Michael.

"If this is the same Roberta, she was the patient that had a profound affect on her leaving medical school. But she died the night before Manerva left. I remember she was so upset with how she had been treated and she felt they just let her die," said Alison.

"I remember also, that Manerva's concern was how powerless she felt that there was nothing she could do to help her or her child? Michael said.

"Child! This is too weird; we must not be talking about the same Roberta because, there were rumors in the laboratory that her urine test showed she was pregnant before she died in surgery that night. But afterwards, I even wondered because I worked in the laboratory at the time. I remember going back because there was never a mention of her ever being pregnant during her surgery or after she had died. I was curious so I went and looked in the laboratory records and there were none. So, this has got to be a different Roberta. Plus all this happened about fifteen years ago," said Bates.

Oh My God! It just can't be...

"Valerie, will you and Brian, go into that empty room across the way now! I'll come and explain to you later and close the door! I'm fine I just need to do something first," Katherine-Jean said as she nervously started shaking and crying trying to explain.

Deanna rushed over to her and put her arms around her.

"Katherine-Jean, didn't you hear what the doctor said, "Manerva, is coming back to us," said Deanna as everyone just looked in amazement. Katherine-Jean, looked up into Deanna's eyes with tears streaming from hers and said, "But you don't understand, God will never forgive me, *I now know who Roberta is! She is Valerie's mother!" said Katherine-Jean. "I never knew until this very moment!"*

"Somebody, get me a wet towel, Katherine-Jean, you need to calm down; you are not making any sense. You are Valerie's mother," Deanna said.

"No, Deanna, I need to tell it all, now I understand why Manerva fainted, she figured it out too, and she was already just too exhausted to digest it all. It was too much for her! That's why she suddenly became too weak and fell! Now it all makes sense! Everything, suddenly makes sense! I did this to Manerva! I will loose my children and they will hate me now! But I never knew until now!" Katherine-Jean said.

"Just slow down, Katherine-Jean," said Dr. Sumner and tell us everything. No body is going to judge you. We are here to help you. "I'm going to go out and be with the children to keep them calm," said Mrs. Sumner. Dr. Parks held a wet towel on her forehead as Deanna gave her a drink of water.

Katherine-Jean, suddenly stopped shaking and looked around at everyone...

"Thanks to all of you, I need to start from the beginning. If any of this will help Manerva then I want to tell you all everything. Michael would you take notes. We may be able to fill in parts. I knew nothing of *a Roberta and still don't but I know what happened to me that hot humid night about fifteen years ago*...Dear God, I need you to help me tell this story!

Just like I told Manerva yesterday...

It all started back when I met Donald in Arkansas in nineteen seventy five, twenty years ago. Everybody here just assumed I had this nice childhood, because of the facade we had worked hard at portraying and keeping up. Happy Upper Class Family. Husband—Caucasian—Successful Business Developer and Entrepreneur, Wife—Black—Beautiful Retired Nurse—Parents of Two Beautiful Children—A Daughter almost sixteen—who want to someday be a Doctor. A Son—almost twelve—who want to someday be just like his Dad. That picture I just painted sounded good, the only problem is it's all a lie. Well, not all of it, the children's dreams are real, that's why this all hurts so.

Donald had nothing, when I met him. I don't know what I must have been thinking. I never knew who my parents were, all my life the parents I thought were mine were not. I loved them and thought they loved me. I grew up an only child, always wanting other brothers and sisters. Anyway, I didn't find out they weren't my real parents until one hot southern night in Arkansas. This was during my fifth year of marriage to Donald. I loved him so and I had tried to be the wife he wanted and the daughter my parents wanted so. So here is the long story Manerva. The truth about it all. And it goes like this...

Once Upon A Time....

To this day I never understood, how they thought telling me I wasn't their real daughter and in the same breathe telling me how they and Donald had arranged for me to become pregnant in the same sentence was going to make me happy. I never knew I had been injected until after I woke up. I was unaware I had been given hot chocolate with sedatives that knocked me completely out. I remember vaguely dreaming of several doctors standing around me. The next morning after I woke up, I remember seeing both my so called parents and Donald sitting beside my bed talking. I remember them asking me how I felt and did I remember anything. I told them I didn't except seeing the doctors. They told me I had been injected with some of Donald's sperms to see if I could become pregnant that way.

We had tried almost everything known unsuccessfully for the previous five years. I remember beginning to feel different after about the third week. I went to the doctor and was told I was pregnant. I became so happy. It didn't take away the hurt of finding out they were not my real parents but it eased the pain to know I would have a child of my own to love. It was not until my doctor showed me later that some of my test results were very different than they had ever been before. I should have looked into it further then but just knowing I was almost in my eight month and about to finally deliver was all that I could think of. It was not until I had a miscarriage two years later that I overheard Donald and my parents talking one night about how thankful they were that he had found some frozen embryo cells whose mother had just become pregnant and had died in surgery or I would never have gotten pregnant.

They were bragging that it was perfect because the mother was black and the father was white and also that the father was one of the doctors who had come that night. They were bragging because they felt they had paid a good price for the implanted frozen embryo cells they had placed in me. One of the doctors knew Donald and how desperate he was for his wife to become pregnant. When I confronted Donald with this, he admitted everything and told me if I ever told or tried to leave him he would divorce me and take my child away because I had signed papers with my parents both as witnesses that same night I remember nothing about. Per Donald the papers stated that he was the natural father that had supplied the sperm and the mother had died in surgery and had wished to remain unknown prior. Donald told me I had signed stating I was only the acting surrogate mother who had volunteered for this rather new In vitro fertilization procedure only. Donald stated he and my parents had all the papers witnessed and notarized that after the baby was born I would give up all rights as an acting surrogate mother and return the child to its natural father who was Donald.

Being a nurse...

I had read articles on this new procedure that really became known about 1978. Several cases had been very successful. I had never thought about it as an option and was unaware Donald or my parents not only had heard of it but had arranged for it to be done and on me. They just used me and my body. The only thing I knew was that even in all the wrong, somehow God had worked his power through me of keeping life. Life to frozen embryo cells that grew within my body and one of those cells had become fertilized and stayed alive within my body. This is all I knew. I guess deep down, this is all I ever wanted to know. I was implanted that night fifteen years ago with frozen embryo cells. I remember having only one feeling the moment life started growing within me, *and that was love.* Nothing else mattered at that point. I never confronted my so called parents since they had paid Donald, signed those papers without telling me or getting my consent and setting up a trust fund for him to have control of all their businesses and money until each of my children became eighteen. They even put in a stipulation to make a game out of it all. I guess they always knew I would care more for my children than their money, so they never gave me any power or say so in the entire situation.

They knew if I ever was in a position to make a choice I would choose my children over the money. So they had it all worked out so Donald would be the one who had control of the trust fund even after my children turned eighteen as long as he remained their father prior to their eighteenth birthday. The only stipulation is if he is proved by law to be unworthy for any reason prior to each child becoming eighteen, then each child will have control of their own trust upon turning eighteen. I guess they figured they gave me and my children eighteen years to fight and play games with him and if we couldn't win over him in eighteen years he deserved it all. I guess they felt they had paid for me maybe the same way and I turned out alright. They got what they paid for with me, so why shouldn't Donald get what he paid for also.

I remember growing up and they would always make me play these competitive games for almost everything. Years later, I thought about some of the rumors I use to hear growing up, that our black maid was my father's mistress. I remember seeing younger pictures of her and thinking she was even more beautiful than Lena Horne. I remember my mother always telling me when I was a child how her own mother had been raped by one of their workers. I guess I always wanted to believe that explained how I could be their daughter and look a lot like Lena Horne as many would say or how two whites could have a mixed black daughter. Nothing else made sense. Nothing was really ever given to me even when I did deserve it.

Over the years of marriage Donald cheated and let me know he would take my daughter, the money and tell her I was not her mother unless I behaved as a wife to him and give him a son. So I just existed giving all my love to my daughter, and I became unfaithful once during my marriage. *During that time I really did become pregnant.* Donald found out I had been unfaithful and blood test were done. It turned out Donald was the real father. This gave him more ammunition against me. There were so many times I had dreamed about just leaving Donald, taking both my children and letting him have all the money. I never did for fear he would find me and out of revenge take them away legally and then take all their money.

About six years ago...

Was about the time his company had almost become bankrupt and I met Mrs. Sumner. He had threatened to take both of my children away, divorce me if I didn't help him get his business back up and running. From then until now all of the rest has been just history. Thank God I became friends with you and Deanna and I have been able to play the part better. I guess I felt I had other things to focus on and things were appearing alright at least for my children anyway. Donald has never loved them but he has been able to present himself as this very busy father totally devoted to his work.

Manerva, yesterday Donald had me served with divorce papers. He only wants a divorce now because Valerie will turn eighteen in less than two years and to eliminate any chance of me ever thinking that I might have any way of ever proving him unworthy he want to get full custody now. With Donald it has always been about the money. He cares nothing for the children. I use to think it was really because Valerie was really not his, but Brian is, and Manerva he cares nothing for Brian either. I don't care about the money, I never have. I want Valerie to know the truth and maybe find and know about her real parents. I owe her that! I'd like to give her what I never had!

I have asked God for forgiveness so many times...

Because I have been selfish in loving my daughter for sixteen years and I couldn't find the strength. It has only been since I met Manerva, that I found the strength to let go and let God. She had encouraged me and loved me knowing only part of the story. I just hope it's not too late.

That's why I went to Manerva's office today, to tell her everything," said Katherine-Jean as she looked into Dr. Sumner's eyes.

"And, you talked to me instead," Dr. Sumner said.

"Yes, sir, you were great, you made me feel reassured. I wanted to tell you everything, but I couldn't, I didn't know how?" Katherine-Jean said.

"In fact, I had made up in my mind to not even tell Manerva everything, but when she called me and asked me where was I and just showed up almost ten minutes later, I knew she needed to know.

Had known all this would happen...

I never would have said a word. I never would have imagined Manerva and I were connected to a fifteen year secret that happened over six hundred miles away," she said.

"You can't blame yourself, we all know Manerva, once she makes her mind up about something, nothing will stop her," said Andrew.

"He's right, our baby girl, must have felt there was more than you had told her, maybe that's why she came to you. I'm sure she had no idea, there could have been any connection or she would have told you herself, but she knew you needed her, just as she needs you right now," said Emma

Chapter Thirteen

Nothing But Good News!

I am just glad to know Manerva will be alright and you have got all our love, support and Roman's money to fight Donald," said Deanna.

We are going to fight Mr. Donald with more than love, support and money...

We are to prove him very unworthy by law in court and way before Valerie turns eighteen," said Michael.

"Bates, Alison, Dr. Sumner, I was taking notes *and have a plan of action.* I just called my office and some friends I know in high places back in Memphis and Arkansas. Could we step outside to talk about it for a minute. Katherine-Jean you just sit and relax and know you will keep your children. Don't say anything to them about any of this, there will be no need to," Michael said with nothing but hope and confidence coming from his words.

"Excuse me, Michael; could we come with you, we have connections with a lot of doctor and business developer friends in Memphis and Arkansas also. My husband personally knows a lot of clubs and groups that Donald belongs to, we would like to help," said Dr. and Mr. Parks.

"Young man, we travel abroad, and have a lot of political friends and judges, that owe us a lot of favors, maybe we could help, said Alison's dad.

"Manerva would be delighted, and so would I, of course, please join us," said Michael.

"May God be with each of you. Our baby girl is going to wake up to nothing but good news!" Andrew shouted!

"Michael, you know you have all my support on this! This is the type of fight I love to be involved in!" said Dr. Sumner.

Michael and his group left to meet...

"Mom, Mrs. Sumner took us and we got some things, out of your suitcase, we know you need and like," said Brian.

"Here are your blue and white warm up suit and your exercise leotards. This hospital is so neat; they have an exercise room, track, racquetball ball court and an indoor pool in the doctor's gallery. Dr. Sumner's gave us his guest pass. Valerie wants to do your hair and nails first. Is it okay if I go and play some racquetball until you and Valerie get there?" asked Brian.

"Are you feeling better? Mrs. Sumner told us you are feeling better. She said with all that has happened, not all people respond the same, and that you were extra tired working with Aunt Manerva all evening. Mom, I've got this really cool makeup and hair kit, I bought. I know just the hair style you need and I'm going to do one for Aunt Manerva, once she gets better. I already did Aunt Deanna earlier tonight. I'd like to do one for you now, if you like?, asked Valerie.

"That sounds great Valerie! I'd love for you to fix me up!" Katherine-Jean said smiling.

"Katherine-Jean I'd love to go to the doctor's gallery with your son said Alison. I need to do some walking for exercise to keep me and the baby in shape. I'll be with him until you and your daughter get there. That will give you two some time together," Alison said smiling.

"That sounds great thanks," said Katherine-Jean.

"I'll be waiting right here until they finish running all those test in my baby girl's room. I see so many people pushing carts and x-ray looking machines in and out," Emma said. "I'll be right here with you honey," Andrew said.

"Bates, could you make sure that door is closed, this is a hospital too, and you never know who may be passing by or listening," Michael said. The Nurse Manager said we could use this office to meet, that way we have our privacy and still close to Manerva's room."

"My office just called me back and is sending me faxes of different lists. I am connected through several political and medical networks through my laptop. There will be names on these lists of all the doctors and patients that were registered at First General Hospital that weekend. Also a list of all of the Board of Trustee Members, Judges, and Business Partners registered through the Chamber of Commerce in Memphis, Arkansas and the surrounding areas fifteen years ago. They are also going to cross reference those names to try to narrow the list down to see if any of those names are on any of the medical record files of patients that were admitted through the Emergency Room, had any surgeries performed as well as died on the weekend that Manerva had told me was her last day before she left Medical School there fifteen years ago and who has a first name of *Roberta.* I'm also checking out all social services and getting a court order to go through and check the signatures on the Katherine Jean's mother and father accounts on the supposedly notarized papers. I've got an idea that could spend this process up. If anyone has any other ideas, throw them out ASAP. Why don't we divide into two groups to go through those lists? Bates, Alison and I go through the list of doctors and patients. Look for any and everything that might give us a connection. Bates you might recognize some names or Alison right off, and especially if they cross reference on another list for an example as a business partner or have a political tie, I may recognize. And all of you can go through the list to see if you see any political, business, or social connections that may connect somehow. Let's all throw out anything we may help. No matter what it is. We all heard Katherine-Jean's story together. The faxes are coming in now, anybody want to throw out anything now, while I'm connecting my portable printer up," Michael said.

"I can't exactly put my finger on it but, I had two meetings earlier today with Manerva and she kept saying she wish she had the power then she has now. This has to do with a case we will have on Monday where the client swears the doctor was negligent and caused the patient to die, but there is no proof. As the medical examiner, I have looked over all the records with a fine tooth comb. All of the records support exactly what the doctors are saying. Manerva commented to me, the records could have been tampered with. It's just my gut feeling, she may have been thinking of this case now the more that I think about it. I think she was already starting to make some connections, said Dr. Parks.

"Doc, since you said that, I remember distinctly the night I met Manerva, I remember telling her, I had over heard several fellow med techs say the patient's urine test showed she was pregnant. But after this same patient died, there was never a mention of any test showing anything about a pregnancy during surgery or after Roberta died in surgery. In fact, I was a little curious and I went to check the lab results again myself, but there was no record and there were no lab results. A couple of pages from our lab log were missing also. I just figured they were in another chart or something. Manerva had left, I didn't know Alison then or that she knew Manerva, so I just let it go. But that whole case didn't feel right to me," said Bates.

"Bates, do you remember any of the doctor's names that worked that night? asked Michael.

"The only one I will never forget is Dr. Grant, who worked the emergency room," Bates said. "Not, Dr. Henry E. Grant Sr.," asked Michael. "No," said Bates. "It was his son is all I remember because rumors were that since Dr. Henry E. Grant was on the hospital board of trustee, his son got away with everything. People were too scared to say anything for fear of loosing their jobs," Bates said.

"That was the doctor's name that was giving Manerva such a hard time, their were also rumors in med school, that he was a womanizer and hated blacks. I was hoping I got him for my intern rotation instead of Manerva, but I didn't. Also, there were other rumors that I never mentioned to anyone especially after Manerva left that Dr. Grant was messing around with another nursing student that worked in the out patient lab. Everybody was talking because she was a black woman and she came to work sometimes with bruises and black eyes. Rumors were did he do it?" Alison said.

"Alison, I heard those same rumors, but I didn't know you at the time. Hey, wait a minute, I know who and where that nursing student lives because she went to my high school," said Bates.

"I just wonder where is that young nursing student and did she ever get pregnant ?" Dr. Sumner said. "We may be able to establish a pattern." Mr. Parks said. "Since Arkansas was near Memphis but in a different jurisdiction, my gut feeling is if we look hard enough in the surrounding area even including Mississippi, we may find all kind of connections. Especially doing that time. I think back at some of the rumors that were talked about in some of the country club meetings with a lot of powerful people," said Alison's dad.

"I think we are on to something big, because Dr. Henry E. Grant was the grandson of the late cotton tycoon, Mitchell Grant. They were one of the most powerful families in the south during that time. Dr. Henry E. Grant ran for Mayor and won the election but just before he was to start serving office, he was mysteriously found shot to death in his home in Arkansas. Years later his son Dr. Mitchell Grant lost his medical license and arrested along with three other doctors and business developers for a big malpractice operation. They were arrested about five years ago and still serving time now. They tried to keep it as quiet as they could because the investigation is still going on. I never discussed it with Manerva because we sort of got out of touch the last five years. Plus there was no reason to tell her about all this," he said.

"Well, you are back in touch now, and no time too soon, Dr. Sumner said.

"I recognize a couple of shaky judges and business names from my political groups," said Alison's dad.

"And I know some of these names that does business with a Donald DeWitt. They are some of the same ones that caused some problems for a lot of people before I became a retired doctor," Mr. Parks said.

"Interesting said Dr. Sumner, that's Katherine-Jean's husband."

"I also recognize her parent's names on the Chamber of Commerce business developers list from Arkansas. I remember

Katherine-Jean telling us when we first met her that they both had just died in a car accident...makes you wonder?" Dr. Sumner said.

"Here is the Dean of Students name on the business list from Memphis that was in the meeting the day he and Dr. Grant met with Manerva on her last day," said Alison.

"I think we have more than enough names to start gathering information," said Bates.

"We have more than that, Bates. Just with you, Alison, Katherine-Jean, Manerva and some key names, we can present an air tight case to prove legally Mr. DeWitt not only be removed from the children and Katherine-Jean's Trust Fund. With just a little more documentation we will be able to have him indicted on conspiracy charges and sent away to serve time for injustice he and Katherine-Jean's parents forced her into," he said.

"He should be in jail a very long time for that. I need several more things investigated, to have all feel right to me. First, I'm not stopping until I find out who were all of the doctors who were there that night to perform the surgery that Roberta died from? Secondly, I need to know who where all of the doctors who went to Katherine-Jean with Mr. DeWitt to perform the implanted surrogacy procedure? Thirdly, I need to have proof that one of those doctors were actually the father of the frozen embryo cells and if not who is? And lastly, I need proof that Roberta was the mother or not? And if so, I need to know did she have relatives?" Michael said.

"I'm not sure about all the doctor's but as for Roberta, a good start may be to check and find out the med tech that worked in the out patient laboratory across from the emergency room on that same day as well as the ones who originally saw the original urine test that showed pregnancy. The one rumor I did know was true was they were friends and she had come up to visit her to talk on her lunch break. The reason I know it was true was because she was fired that same day. I figured she either told something or knew something?" said Bates.

"Bingo!" said Michael.

"We have connections on how we can find out the list of doctors that performed the surgery on Roberta and pronounced her dead, and get all the records," Dr. Parker said. "We are almost positive once we have that list, some of those same names will show up on your business list from Arkansas," said Mr. Parker.

"Another Bingo! I'm going to get some people in social service checking into any the means and list of contacts they can find on how one would be able to obtain a baby or frozen embryo cells at that time legal or illegally," Michael said.

"Let's have all the court records look into all of Katherine-Jean parents personal and business papers including wills, birth certificates, trust, all business contracts, etc, I'm curious to read the exact papers Katherine-Jean signed and see the names on them too. I agree, I'm almost sure some of those same names will show up on them also," Dr. Sumner said.

"Well, we've been in here almost an hour for our meeting. Today is Friday, by Monday; I should have everything we need to have Mr. DeWitt arrested. It's going to feel good to be able to not only be able to tell Manerva that we have worked her fifteen year case for her, but to be able to tell Katherine-Jean who Valerie's biological mom and dad is as well as her own real parents," said Michael.

"Instead of Katherine-Jean thinking she or Valerie will loose anything, it will be the complete opposite and at the same time they both discover not only do they have each other but they each will have an additional set of grandparents from an additional mom that they each can be proud of to know they were once *really loved* and only because of circumstances beyond their control did they have to give them up. This will be the kind of *news I know Manerva will wake up and smile about," said Michael.*

" I need to go and make all of the calls to cancel the banquet for tomorrow night," Dr. Sumner said.

"No, Dr. Sumner, you are not going to cancel the banquet. We are all practically here anyway. We will just have it in Manerva's room instead of some fancy ballroom down the street. This will still be Manerva's Night. I didn't come all the way here to not tell Manerva all the wonderful things she deserves to hear. Of how she has done so much good for others. This is a prime example right here. Look at how many different people lives have been touched by Manerva's spirit of helping here tonight. I've let the past five years slip away. I'm not wasting any more time," Michael said.

Deanna had been out with Katherine-Jean and Valerie for a while. Then she went in with Andrew and Emma to be with Manerva for awhile. *She had quietly come inside the meeting room, and heard about half of the meeting. In her own little world, all of today had really affected her as well. Her two best friends, Katherine-Jean and Manerva were like the sisters she never had. She was trying to stay strong for them. She watched as she looked at both her friends, knowing neither of them would be the same again.*

Manerva, would eventually wake up and be okay, all her tests showed that it was merely a matter of time. Deanna knew God had answered another prayer just like Manerva had always told them he would and worked another miracle through all of them. God had worked his power through using Manerva to bring everyone together. She didn't know anyone else that could have brought so many different people together. From different walks of life. And bring them in a small room with nothing but each other and from it come nothing but love. Deanna knew it was God!

A new baby was announced to be born. A togetherness of people that had for whatever reason gotten caught up in the fast lane of life. What could have been described by many as an emergency crisis or a bad thing was merely a blessing from God. Deanna knew Manerva's parents strength, love and prayers is what this was all about. They always knew deep down Manerva was just resting, in a way she was just resting for God as they put it.

Who would ever have imagined that a fifteen year old secret for one person and a mere feeling for another would not only be discovered but discussed and solved within six hours? That also was a miracle from God.

Katherine-Jean will be better and stronger because she will truly be able to let go now and let God because there are no more hidden secrets. The biggest realization from her is to know the love you felt from her heart and from inside her womb over fifteen years ago was true love. It didn't matter whether it is labeled biological or by being a surrogate, it is love and it represents life. How can she be judged, she was never given a choice? She never even knew. Her only choice would have been to deny a life that had started growing within her womb. How could she have denied life? For her there was never a question, only an answer. And she chose the right answer. To allow the life that had started to continue because it is a blessing from God.

For me, I sit her just smiling, I feel as though I am lying in my bed, because I feel Roman so. He feels me also. This I now know through all of this because he is living more with me now, than he did when I could touch him. I think because, we are now able to live within each other everywhere and all the time. It was Roman within me that had already provided all of the means to coordinate and get everyone here before they knew they needed to be here. Even before I knew we all needed to be here.

It is still that same Roman within me that just gave Michael the financial support he needed for his campaign and to put closure to this fifteen year secret for Manerva so she can wake up and be free. It is that same freedom I now feel, like my grandmother Anna. That same freedom my brother felt when he hugged me the night before he was killed in the car accident with both of the people he loved. I'm not saying he knew he would be killed. But now I know when Toney hugged and kissed me and told me he loved me and that I was such a special person and I just deserved to be loved. Now, I know what he meant, it was a freedom he felt. He finally felt his worth and it didn't matter what happened next.

Now, I understand when you reach that point, you can really see everything clearly. Nothing and nobody clouds your vision. You can look at past events and understand them more. You can look to the future with an overwhelming desire that if you give of yourself to the best of your ability the outcome doesn't matter because there was nothing more you could have done. Now I know that is the point Manerva use to tell me, "Deanna, my mom and dad always told me, you just wait and see, if you live right, right will follow you. You will get to a point that you have gone as far as you can go, and if you believe in him then you come into God and then you can let go and let God. Everything will just start to feel right. It will just feel good!"

As Deanna stood smiling thinking from within and looking out as Manerva's doctors...

Were all around working with her. Standing beside her were both of Manerva's parents hugging and holding one another as tears of joy silently ran down both their cheeks.

Being a doctor myself, I knew how miraculously this all was. Medically speaking, we couldn't explain it.

By now, as others had slowly heard that Manerva was slowly coming back around she had a group of people that loved her standing looking around, as the doctors looked up smiling as she slowly moved one finger, then one arm, then one leg and so on.

There was one last concern and all of Manerva's doctors agreed upon it. It was not to take the eye patches from her eyes too early. Since Manerva's parents had informed them that there was a high history of diabetes that ran on both sides of their families. They had placed eye drops and were performing additional testing to make sure all would be alright once she opened her eyes to the light.

Chapter Fourteen

We Will Talk And See For You!

Everybody was smiling and hold hands now...

It appeared Manerva was able to slowly move all limbs, the doctors were all leaving. They had informed them earlier that the last two things would be her speech and sight and they didn't want to rush them. They would both come back naturally at the right time.

After all of Manerva's doctors and hospital personnel left her room, Michael beckoned for everyone to come into her room. Everyone was in awe of what he was going to say or do but Dr. Sumner pushed a stool over so he was close to Manerva.

"Dr. Sumner. I know all the doctor's said we could come in and talk to Manerva, and that could probably speed up her recovery. I know it's only about eleven o'clock on a snowy Friday Chicago morning, and I know everybody have millions of things they need to be doing but do you think we could all take a few more minutes out and have the Award Banquet done now instead of tomorrow night? There are some things I want Manerva to hear now. I know all of the guest are not here but the people that matter are, Michael said in the most sincere tone.

"Michael, considering all, I think that would be an excellent idea and quite appropriate," Dr. Sumner said.

"Thanks, would everybody come in close so we could close the door and join hands first. Mr. Jones would you lead us in a moment of prayer first. I'll hold Manerva's hand on this side," said Michael.

"I'll hold my Dollbaby's other hand on this side," said Emma.

So, after Andrew delivered a very heart felt prayer...

Thanking God for all, Michael sort of looked at me and I acted as the mistress of ceremony announcing that we were all here to celebrate someone special. I announced that the award was originally scheduled for tomorrow which would be Saturday night. I went on to say that due to someone we all love having an unforeseen accident on yesterday turned out to *be a miraculous blessing for each of us as we all came here to this hospital.* I then looked back at Michael and he gave me a nod of approval and I knew to just say it.

So today, we are all here instead of on tomorrow night to honor and celebrate a wonderful person, I personally hold near and dear to my heart. A person that our friend *Congressman Michael C. Glenn* from Memphis, TN flew in to be our guest speaker. At this point I looked at Michael and said, "Michael you have the floor, take it away!"

Michael then, sat down slowly on the stool next to the bed while still holding Manerva's right hand and spoke directly to her. "It is with great pleasure that I announce that the person we are all here to honor and celebrate for their achievements and accomplishments is none other than *Manerva R. Jones.* Manerva, we have so much to tell you about so much. I don't want to bombard you with too much detail now. So all I will say is don't you worry about anything.

Listen up good Manerva because we all want you to hear what I am about to say. *You helped us figure out who Roberta was and justice will be done on all levels. I have just received word from my office that several judges in Memphis and in Arkansas will be issuing subpoenas starting on Monday. This is all our battle and we are fighting with you and for you. You didn't know but Dr. Grant lost his license to practice medicine years ago, he is serving time now, and several judges feel we have enough evidence for what he did to you as well as Katherine-Jean to keep him in jail for a very long time and some other people will be joining him soon.*

Enough about all that...

We wanted you to believe this celebration was for Dr. Sumner. He is a wonderful person and a man that we all admire also. But I want you to hear me tell you this *Award Banquet Celebration* has been for you from the start. Only for you! We all love you Manerva. We all appreciate you! " Michael said.

"Look, Michael, tears are falling from her eyes underneath her eye pads. She hears you!" said Emma.

"Manerva, don't worry about anything. I Love you! I have always loved you! Please forgive me that it has taken so long for me to realize you are the only person for me. Manerva, I have a speech I had already prepared to give tomorrow night in your honor. If it's okay with you I would like to give it now, just squeeze my hand with your right hand if you hear me and you want to hear my speech?" he said.

Emma grabbed her mouth and everyone had there eyes watching as Manerva slowly closed her right hand around Michael's hand squeezing it. As Michael slowly pushed the stool away and got on one knee, he said, my speech is very simple and short,

"Manerva R. Jones, will you marry me?

At that moment...

And in total amazement to all Manerva slowly pulled her left arm over and felt her way until she grabbed and placed her left hand squeezing Michael's left arm.

"Manerva, if that is a yes, then I have placed my left hand next to your left hand, then squeeze it now," Michael said.

With all the strength Manerva seemed to have she grabbed Michael's left hand into hers squeezing it in addition to still squeezing his right hand.

For a brief moment there was nothing but silence in the room...

There was not a dry eye in the room. Having both of Manerva's hands in both of his and still down on his knees Michael lifted his head up and looked up into Andrew's eyes, saying, "Sir, I know this is not how most would imagine this moment to be, but I love your daughter, and promise to always be good to her. I promise to cherish her for as long as I live. I will be her mouth and her eyes and all that she could ever need. I'm asking, may I have your daughter's hand in marriage?

Andrew looked over at Emma as she nodded in approval. Andrew then went and bent over and kissed Manerva on her forehead and asked, "Baby girl, you know me and your mama just want you to be happy, Is this what you really want? Show me some sign.

As Emma walked over and kissed her also, Manerva raised her right knee up and let it slowly go back down.

Andrew then looked back at Michael and said, "Yes you may, we would be proud to have you as a son. Our babygirl just gave us a sign. We were just wondering what took you so long?" he said smiling.

"Then Sir, would you do us the honor and perform the ceremony now? We can have a big fancy wedding later, but for now, I came to Chicago tonight not to attend an award banquet but for the *sole purpose* of proposing and asking Manerva to marry me? And we have everyone here Manerva and I would want to be here, plus I know both my parents are smiling looking down from heaven with their blessing," said Michael.

"Son, just a minute, I need to go and get...

Before Andrew could finish his sentence a voice from out of no where quickly interrupted him and said, "Here is what you need!"

Deanna had gotten the charge nurse to page the Hospital Chaplin stat when she got that "gut" feeling he may do this.

"Would you perform the ceremony, I'd like to do something I've never done before, I'd like to stand next to my daughter and give her away," Andrew said reaching for his handerkerchief.

"Deanna, Katherine-Jean, Alison, Dr. Parks and Valerie would you be her Maid of Honor and Bride Maids," asked Emma. They each nodded quickly and moved on the side next to Emma.

"Dr. Sumner, Mr. Parks, Bates and Brian would you be my Best Man and Groomsmen," asked Michael. They nodded quickly and moved on the side next to Michael.

Michael then looked out at Alison's mom and dad and asked, "Would you both be our witnesses. They quickly nodded and stood at the foot of the bed.

"Mrs. Sumner, I would be honored if you would stand next to Dr. Sumner and both of you fill in for my mom and dad for me," asked Michael. She looked with happiness in her face and moved close to her husband.

"There's one thing missing, let's find something to be the ring so we can get started," said the Hospital Chaplin.

"No need to do that, I've got the real thing, this was my mom's wedding ring, this is all I have of her. I brought it hoping and praying Manerva would agree to marry me. This was really going to be my speech as guest speaker on Saturday! When Manerva is all well we can go shopping and she can pick the ring of her choice when we re-new our vows at our big fancy wedding," said Michael smiling.

"That's something old, I've got something borrowed and here's something blue," said Emma.

"Then let's have us a wedding in the name of Jesus," Andrew said.

There were smiles and tears of joy inside and outside the hospital room. The entire hospital and waiting area was like a fantasy for those brief moments. It was as though God stopped everything except the wedding. People were standing all around looking in.

My ceremony was great and the highlight everybody thought was when my dad kept repeating many of the lines along with the Hospital Chaplin from memory of the ceremony and mom I couldn't see but I could feel giving him glances and nods several times to just let the poor Chaplin do the ceremony. After that didn't work, I smiled because I heard my mom fussing at dad in a soft whisper to just shut up!

But I think everyone's ultimate highlight came from hearing me speak softly and clearly lying on this hospital bed for the very first time while holding my true love's hand and answering as loud as I could, "I do!"

Printed in the United States
45779LVS00002B/115

9 781424 107063